WITCH SLAPPED

A BEECHWOOD HARBOR MAGIC MYSTERY
BOOK THREE

DANIELLE GARRETT

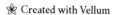 Created with Vellum

BOOKS BY DANIELLE GARRETT

BEECHWOOD HARBOR MAGIC MYSTERIES

Murder's a Witch

Twice the Witch

Witch Slapped

Witch Way Home

Along Came a Ghost

Lucky Witch (Fall 2017)

BEECHWOOR HARBOR GHOST MYSTERIES

The Ghost Hunter Next Door

Ghosts Gone Wild

INTRODUCTION

Holly's got a big problem.
And this time, there's no dead body involved.
At least, not yet.
Her boyfriend's parents are coming into town for the Yule
Feast and they're staying at the Beechwood Manor -- for an
entire week!
With a paranormal meet-the-parents on the horizon, the last
thing she needs is to stumble into yet another murder
investigation, but when she becomes a key witness, there's no
way of avoiding it. Especially not if vampires are involved
and her human partner-in-sleuthing is racing right into
their path.
Holly has to stop a ring of power-hungry vampires, charm a
pair of uptight shifters, and keep herself out of supernatural
prison. Piece of cake, right?

$\mathcal{W}$inter in Beechwood Harbor was a beautiful time of year, despite the weather that tended to fluctuate between peaceful, crisp days with no wind or rain and days with miniature monsoons that made it feel more like a ghost town. All the shops were decked out with twinkling lights and festive displays, and most every house had some kind of decorations on display. In the center of town, a huge Christmas tree was adorned with soft twinkle lights and glowing ornaments. Even the Beechwood Manor had its own Christmas tree sparkling in the front window. Adam, Evangeline, and I had trekked into the woods behind the manor and spent hours debating which tree would look the best. After all, it would be showcased front and center for the entire neighborhood to see.

Everyone in town was electrified with the spirit of the holidays. Not to mention that the tip jar at Siren's Song was overflowing by the end of each day. There was only one real complication: Yule Feast was on the horizon and Adam and I were about to venture into unchartered territory in our relationship. I had yet to meet his parents and it was a conversation I'd been dreading for weeks. Now that the time was drawing near, the stress was almost tangible, like the tingling in the air right before a lightning storm. I knew it was on the way and sure enough, one Wednesday night after a cozy dinner for two at McNally's, it hit.

"My dad called today," Adam said conversationally as we wandered down the street. We were taking advantage of a break in the rainy weather that had plagued the harbor for the past week. The rain had finally let up and moved farther up the coastline. It was still freezing cold, but with the right amount of bundling into coats and gloves and scarves, we were able to resume our usual practice of taking a post-dinner walk around town.

I cringed slightly. "Oh, yeah? How are they doing?"

Adam rubbed his gloved hands together, trying to get them warm again. "Same old, I guess. Dad's up for a promotion at work. I told him he's getting a little too old to be chasing bad guys down." Adam paused and grinned at the memory. "He didn't appreciate that."

I laughed lightly. "I wouldn't think so."

"Apparently he's going to remind me that he's still the Big Bad Wolf next time he's in town."

I smiled and shook my head. "That should be quite the showdown." I hadn't met Adam's wolf-shifter father, but I imagined that he'd been the one to teach Adam most of what he knew, and in beast form, Adam was quite intimidating. That is, when he wasn't pilfering around in McNally's day-old garbage, scarfing down as much discarded pub food as he could stuff into his muzzle.

"Well from the sound of it, you'll get front row seats," Adam replied. He glanced at me out of the corner of his eye. "I invited them for Yule Feast."

My stomach flipped over and curled in on itself. "You did?"

Adam gave an easy shrug. "I thought they might like coming out to see the town and the manor. And, of course, meet you."

My mouth went dry. "Oh," I said, trying to manage a smile. "That will be nice."

"Is that really so bad?" Adam fixed his dark eyes on me, giving me the you're-not-getting-off-that-easy stare. "I mean, you look like you just swallowed a lemon or something."

"I like lemons," I hedged.

He groaned. "Holly."

"Sorry," I hurried to say. "It's not *bad*. I just wasn't planning a big thing for Yule Feast. You know, I thought maybe we'd stick to one big bash on Christmas day when everyone can come." We'd done a similar event for Thanksgiving, with Nick, Cassie, Kirra, and Chief Lincoln. It had been a lot of fun and I'd secretly been hoping to gloss over Yule Feast, mostly to avoid the exact scenario Adam was proposing.

Adam scrubbed a hand over his sharp jaw line. "Listen, Holly, this is all new for me too. I just thought—"

"Adam," I interjected, stopping in the middle of the sidewalk. I grabbed his arm and tugged him to a stop beside me, looking him in the eye. "It's not a bad thing. I swear."

He glanced down, breaking eye contact. "I probably should have asked you first."

My heart twisted at his dejected tone. I burrowed into his side as we walked, then smiled up at him. "It'll be fine," I said.

"You're sure you don't want me to cancel?"

I shook my head and forced a smile for his benefit. "I'm sure."

We continued our walk, winding through downtown past all the closed-up shops. Evangeline's day spa, The Emerald, was still open, and the glittering marquee sign bathed the street with light. I spotted Lacey through the front window.

"Aha, I see it's Fright Night at the spa," Adam quipped, jutting his chin in Lacey's direction.

I elbowed him playfully in the ribs. "Be nice. You and Lacey have been getting along fabulously, at least for you two, since Thanksgiving. And believe me—the rest of us would like that trend to continue."

"Yeah, yeah." Aside from eating, torturing our vampire roommate was one of his favorite past times. He almost took it to an art form.

Evangeline, our witch roommate, had opened her spa a few months ago when she decided to stay in Beechwood Harbor permanently. Since then, it had grown large enough that she now offered extended hours, which were mostly geared toward the after-work crowd. It was also convenient for Lacey and her vampire friends, who weren't able to pop in during the daytime for obvious reasons.

"You want to go in and say hello?" I asked Adam.

He grimaced at me. "Not a chance. Last time I was in, Evie started telling me she had a new shampoo to treat my receding hairline. She told me that it was best to get a jump on it at a young age."

I stifled a giggle. "She might have started off as a TV star, but she's a natural-born salesperson."

Adam ran a protective hand over his thick, dark hair—which, for the record, definitely didn't need a boost from any kind of shampoo. "Yeah, well she needs to learn to pick her marks a little better. My hair is perfect," he replied, offended.

I rolled my eyes up to the night sky, pleading with the moon for mercy. "Yeah, yeah, you and Lacey could have some kind of hair-off."

"Please tell me that's not a real thing," he said.

I laughed and popped up on my toes to press a quick kiss to his lips. "Don't worry. You'd totally win."

Adam grinned at me—a kiss was usually enough to get

him to quit griping—and ran a finger down the side of my cheek. "Go say hi to the girls, but don't leave me hanging for too long. I don't want that to be the only kiss I get tonight."

A sizzle of heat spread over my skin. "Deal."

I jogged off across the street as Adam started up the hillside that led back to Beechwood Manor. I paused at the door of the spa and watched him disappear into the darkness. He was so good to me—and *for* me. So why was I holding back and so scared of letting him get closer? There were dozens of girls in town that would be thrilled to be dating Adam St. James. They would dream of the day he'd invite them to meet his parents for the official stamp of approval. For me, though, the idea was more terrifying than thrilling. Would I ever be able to get beyond my past and move toward some kind of future?

With a heavy sigh, I tucked the tumultuous thoughts as far into the deepest recesses of my mind as I could and pulled open the door of Evangeline's shop.

The bright lights and upbeat music went a long way toward banishing the dark musings and when Evangeline popped up from her seat at the front counter, I managed a genuine smile. She was decked out in a festive ensemble of a red pencil skirt and a green cashmere sweater. The colors looked even richer against her caramel skin and her bright, smiling eyes. Evangeline had a wardrobe that most women would kill for and always looked put-together. Even her pajama sets matched—and most were made from brightly colored silk to boot.

She waved me inside, her gold feather earrings tinkling beneath her long, raven locks. "Holly! I didn't know you were coming in tonight!"

Lacey was perusing a stand of lotions but turned when Evangeline greeted me, shifting her platinum blonde locks over her shoulder. "Hey, Holly."

"Hello, ladies. Adam and I were walking through the neighborhood and I thought I'd come in and say hello."

Evangeline leaned to the right, glancing past me. "Where's Adam?"

"He went back to the manor."

Evangeline folded her arms, looking one second short of stamping her foot. "Is he *still* upset about my offer to give him some free shampoo samples?"

"Apparently you really did a number on his ego," I said with a giggle.

She heaved her eyes to the ceiling with a dramatic sigh. "Shifters ..."

"Tell me about it."

Evangeline dropped her arms and waved a hand, beckoning me further into the shop. When she'd transformed the abandoned gardening store into a day spa, she'd turned the storage room in the back into three decent-sized treatment rooms that were now hidden behind a long, emerald curtain. The front of the shop was set up with display cases featuring all kinds of different concoctions. She stocked everything from fancy shampoos and soaps to at-home wax kits.

As the owner, Evangeline worked full-time at the store and also employed an esthetician, Lucy, who also happened to be one of my customers, a telepath who used my potions to block her mother-in-law's unflattering, *incessant* internal monologue anytime she's in town for a visit—which, unfortunately for Lucy, is often. Evangeline's other employee was a strapping werewolf named Ben, a masseuse who was *very* popular with the area's female population, including—I suspected—Evangeline herself.

Lucy and Ben were likely already gone for the night as appointments were usually wrapped up earlier in the evening. Since Lacey and Evangeline were the only ones in the front room, Evangeline kicked her feet up on the reservations desk, showcasing a pair of ruby red stilettos that probably cost more than I made in a month. Evangeline raised a hand to cover a wide yawn. "Whew! Sorry." She shook her head. "Why does Siren's Song close so early? I could really use a double shot."

I smiled and sank down onto the sleek black couch that was sandwiched between two product display cases. A glass coffee table sat in front of it, holding a neatly organized array of magazines. "What you need is some sleep," I countered. "You're turning into Cassie. You two could form some kind of sixty-hour-a-week club. Sickos."

Evangeline laughed. "I know. It's a little out of control. I'm debating whether or not I should be closed one day a week. I think Lucy and Ben are about to mutiny if their schedules don't die down a little."

Lacey shot Evangeline a sly grin. "Oh, you know Ben would do anything you asked."

I glanced back at Evangeline as she shrugged off Lacey's comment, but she couldn't seem to mask a wide smile. "Oh, really? Come on, spill."

Evangeline laughed. "There's nothing to tell."

"*Yet*," Lacey added, setting down the bottle in her hand. She crossed the shop and sat beside me on the couch.

"He is pretty yummy," I said, smiling over at Evangeline. "Even by movie star standards."

"First of all, I'm no longer an actress and I was never a movie star." Evangeline rolled her eyes. "And second, I never said he *wasn't* attractive. I merely said that as his boss, I have an obligation to keep things professional."

"I'd fire him if that's the only thing standing in the way," Lacey said, unflinching.

I laughed. "I think if she did that, she'd lose half of her clients. You wanna talk about a mutiny ..."

"Holly's got a point," Evangeline said. "His backside and

7

quote-unquote magic fingers are the best advertising I never had to pay for."

We all dissolved into giggles.

"His schedule is tricky, though," Evangeline said. "That whole once-every-full-moon thing is exhausting."

"How long has he been a werewolf?" I asked. Ben came into Siren's Song a few times a week, so we'd had our fair share of interactions, but I'd never managed to get much information out of him. He seemed to prefer keeping to himself. But surely Evangeline knew his story. He'd been working at The Emerald for a few months. That was plenty of time for her to dig up some dirt.

"A few years," Evangeline answered, dropping her feet to the floor. "He hasn't told me how he was turned, though."

I nodded. It was a fairly common story. Most werewolves were very private and liked to blend into human communities rather than live inside the haven system. I turned to Lacey. "You approve of this union? Don't vamps usually avoid werewolves?"

"Only the ones who act like beasts on the days they *aren't* wearing their fur," she answered, her nose turning up slightly. "Ben doesn't seem like *that* kind of werewolf."

Evangeline waved her hand through the air. "Enough about Ben. What's going on with you and Adam?"

My heartbeat picked up again, slamming back into the same cadence as when Adam brought up our new Yule plans. "What do you mean?" I asked, my voice too thin.

Evangeline hitched a shoulder. "How are things going? You never give us the gossip, girl."

Lacey reached forward and snagged a magazine from the coffee table, clearly uninterested.

I sighed heavily. "He just told me that his parents are coming to town for the Yule Feast."

"Oh?" Evangeline said, her lips forming a small *O*.

Even Lacey looked up from her magazine.

As I'd feared, this was a much, much bigger deal than I wanted it to be. I dragged in a sigh, trying to slow my frantic heart. "I'm not sure I can talk him out of it."

"Talk him out of it?" Evangeline's eyebrows knit together. "Why would you want to do that?"

I glanced at my interlocked fingers in my lap. "I just think it's too big of a step. I mean, they don't even live here. If they did, I wouldn't think of it as such a big deal. Maybe." On second thought, I was pretty sure that geography didn't matter.

"Holly, honey, this is a *good* thing," Evangeline said, her voice soft, as though she realized she was dealing with a flight risk. "Adam's crazy about you. You're crazy about him. It's a natural next step in your relationship."

I glanced at Lacey and then at Evangeline, feeling like I'd been tossed overboard and couldn't reach the lifesaver. "Then why does it feel so incredibly terrifying?"

"Are you worried his parents won't like you?" Evangeline asked.

"Or that they *will?*" Lacey added pointedly before I could answer.

"That's not it," Evangeline told Lacey with a disbelieving laugh. But her eyes widened when she looked back at me. "Is it?"

I shook my head, not sure which part I was denying. "I'm sure it will all be fine. I'm probably over-thinking it."

Evangeline didn't look convinced. "Holly ..."

I quickly cut her off before she could press me further. "I'm not sure how I feel about it. It just happened. I haven't had time to process yet. That's all."

They shared a doubtful glance but let it slide.

I pushed up from the couch and slipped my hands back into my gloves, preparing for the frosty night air. "It'll be fine," I insisted, more to convince myself than my friends. "Besides, you'll both be there if I start tanking, right?"

Evangeline offered a gentle smile. "Of course we will."

Lacey nodded, not looking up from her magazine.

"Then I don't need to worry." I forced a smile before making my way back to the front doors. "See you both at home."

They called out their goodbyes as I pushed out into the night, more confused than ever.

CHAPTER 2

A few days passed and no one brought up the rapidly approaching Yule Feast. It would take place on the night of the Winter Solstice and was somewhat of a paranormal Thanksgiving, minus the football game. We'd all share a large feast, with an assortment of traditional dishes, and there would be music and dancing—and usually a fair amount of rum-laced spiced cider—to follow. The plans for the feast were already in the works, and while there was a lot to be done in the weeks leading up to the event, I was so busy that I didn't have much time to stress out.

Thanks to the success of my potion business, I'd been able to drop back to three shifts a week at Siren's Song, the local coffee shop that my best friend Cassie managed. Paisley, another girl who worked with us, had quit her part-time job at Thistle, the town's natural grocery store, to take my full-time spot. Cassie's younger sister, Kirra, also helped out while she was on winter break from the local community college.

Even with the reduction in my work hours at the coffee shop, I ended up working more hours overall as I spent my days off in the manor's kitchen, whipping up batch after batch of my custom-blend potions. Saturdays were no exception, and with a steady rain thrumming away on the roof and windows, I was glad I didn't have to hoof it the handful of blocks to Siren's Song. Boots, my oversized tabby cat, was glad too. He liked having me around the house more often, although I suspected that had something to do with the copious amounts of treats I handed out to keep him occupied while I worked.

"One more, Bootsie, and then you're officially cut off," I said, dropping a round, kibble-sized treat to the floor beside my foot. I gave it a swift kick and smiled as he scrambled over the hardwood floors to track it down. I started cutting up my next batch of herbs, fresh from the greenhouse, and winced as I heard a solid *thwap*. I peeked over the counter and saw Boots shaking his head, apparently recovering from bashing it into a chair during his pursuit.

I sighed and grabbed another treat from the ceramic container beside the microwave and crossed the kitchen. I stooped down and fed him the new treat before fishing the lost one from behind the potted fern in the corner. "Bootsie, you really need to work on your course-correction skills," I said, stroking his silky head. "Poor little guy."

A voice bellowed from the other side of the door, "Holly?"

"In here!" I called out, pushing off the floor.

Adam swept into the kitchen. "Oh, sorry. I didn't know you were working," he said, eying the assortment of potion ingredients scattered over the L-shaped counter. My trusty green kettle simmered on the stove, warmed by a magically-enhanced blue flame that allowed perfect temperature control.

"Just trying to get caught up," I said, going back to my cutting board. I continued chopping and dicing my way through a pile of rare mushrooms, not looking up even as I felt Adam's gaze on me. "What are you up to?"

"I just finished a conference call with that media company I've been consulting for," he said before dropping into one of the chairs around the farm-style kitchen table. I glanced up and saw him lean over and absently pat Boots on the head. A smile twitched at my lips. The two of them had become quite close over the past few months. "Did you know that we're getting a new roommate?" he asked, looking up at me.

My knife went still, poised over the mushrooms. "No?"

Posy, the ghost that ran the Beechwood Manor, always made a point to hold family-style meetings whenever there were changes in our living arrangements. I'd just spoken with her over breakfast and she hadn't said anything about a new roommate. Adam must have misunderstood.

"Why do you think we're getting a new roommate?"

Adam straightened in his chair and Boots retreated to his cat bed by the back door. "I just saw someone in the sitting room talking to Posy, and noticed he had a big suitcase with him."

"But we don't have a room free. Unless someone is moving out. You don't think someone is moving out, do you?" My eyebrows furrowed together and I set my knife down. I wasn't going to be able to concentrate until I got to the bottom of whatever was going on. "You didn't talk to him?"

"No, but I heard Posy welcome him to the manor." He pushed up and crossed to the fridge. "I think she called him Harvey. Maybe he's just a friend who needed someplace to crash for a night?"

My spine went ramrod straight. "Harvey?" I repeated, slowly turning on my heel to face him.

He gave a quick nod and pushed up from the chair. "Yeah.

Some kind of goblin if I picked up the scent right," he said casually before ducking into the fridge in search of a snack.

The knife in my hand clattered to the counter. "Bats!" I picked up the knife and tossed it into the sink before scrambling to clear away the freshly filled potion vials. If that was the Harvey that I suspected, I needed to get rid of any evidence. My potion making wasn't *exactly* legal.

Adam whirled toward me, the fridge door slamming shut behind him. As I rushed around the kitchen hiding the proof of my work, he looked at me like I'd lost my mind. "What are you *doing?*"

"I don't have time to explain. Just—help! This all has to go away. Right now!"

Without further comment, Adam jumped into action and gathered up a basketful of vials and stashed it under the sink while I extinguished the flame under the kettle on the stove, slammed a lid over the contents, and swept the leftover ingredients into the trash can. Just as we got the counter cleared, the kitchen door swung open and, sure enough, Harvey Colepepper, my assigned SPA agent, was standing there, his elongated nose barely level with the counter.

He gave a sharp smile, his too-pointy teeth on full display. "Holly!"

Adam took a sidestep closer to me and the energy of the room shifted. His protective stance felt like a physical wave of air blowing through the room.

If Harvey noticed, he didn't care. His smile remained firmly in place. I swallowed the lump in my throat and tried to think not-guilty thoughts. "Hello, Harvey. I wasn't expecting you ..."

He laughed, the sound deep and off-putting. I wasn't sure what was more terrifying: Harvey when he was angry or when he appeared too happy. A dozen scenarios raced through my mind. Had one of my customers snitched on me to the Haven Council? Was Harvey here to drag me back to the Seattle haven and throw me back in the dank cell I'd had the misfortune of spending a night in over a year ago? Were there backup SPA agents out front, hiding in the hedges surrounding the property, or crawling through the woods out back? And somewhere amid all the other thoughts, one loomed more terrifyingly than the others: Had Gabriel managed to escape from prison?

A shudder passed over me and Adam set a large, steadying hand at the small of my back. Only then could I manage a full breath before asking, "What are you doing here? In Beechwood Harbor?"

Posy gave me a disapproving look. "Really, Holly. That is no way to talk to a guest. Mr. Colepepper is here—"

"Please," Harvey interrupted, holding up a gnarled finger. "As I said before, you can call me Harvey. I see no need for such formality as this is not official business."

Not official business? The words echoed through my head. Then what was he doing here? Sure, Beechwood Harbor was a lovely town, but it wasn't exactly a top-ten destination. But then what was he doing here? Surely it wasn't a social call. Harvey and I weren't exactly *friendly*. He'd helped me out of my scrape back in the Seattle haven, but on the other hand, he was also the one who'd banished me from my home.

Harvey's inky eyes shifted to lock with mine. I had the distinct feeling he was trying to decipher my thoughts. "I'm staying at the manor while I investigate a local SPA matter."

A mix of confusion, relief, and anxiety coursed through me before colliding and forming a tight knot in my stomach.

"What kind of matter?" Adam asked, not bothering to introduce himself.

Harvey's cold eyes flicked to Adam, who towered over him by at least three feet. If Harvey was intimidated by

Adam's size, he didn't show it. His thin lips curled back into a sneer. "That's none of your concern, Mr. St. James."

Adam blinked and glanced over at me, clearly unnerved that Harvey knew his name. Was Adam on Harvey's radar? And if so, was it because of me?

Harvey looked up at Posy, his expression thawing slightly. "May I be shown to my room?"

"Of course, Mr.—" she paused, before correcting herself, "Harvey. Right through here. We'll take the stairs. I have a lovely room for you on the second floor."

Harvey followed Posy, listening as she went on about the manor, but right before leaving the kitchen, he glanced back and circled the room with his beady eyes, as though looking for something out of place. He gave me a final glance and then he was gone.

I released a shaky breath and glanced down at the counter, only just realizing my hands were gripping the edge so tightly that my knuckles were white.

"Holly, who in the Otherworld was *that?*" Adam asked, keeping his voice low.

I forced myself to pry my fingers off of the counter and stooped down to grab the basket we'd stashed under the sink. "We need to get all of this out of here. Now!"

Basket in hand, I turned and spotted the kettle. "Grab that!"

Adam did as I asked and we scurried out the back door, making a beeline for my greenhouse. It was the one place that I knew Posy wouldn't go when giving her standard tour of the manor and its grounds. The greenhouse was my space and she respected my privacy. I'd been the one to bring the space back from the dead when I first moved in and found it boarded shut, with caked-on dust and cobwebs coating every surface. I'd worked hard to put my stamp on it, and my roommates respected it as my own turf.

When we were inside, I shut the door and applied a ward, sealing it closed. I leaned over the central table, my chest heaving as my heart pounded frantically against it.

"Okay, Holls, what's going on?" Adam asked. "Why are you so freaked out right now?"

I peered out the greenhouse window, staring up at the manor. A light shone from the window of the heretofore empty storage room that sat at the end of the hallway. When had Posy converted that to a guest room? And how?

Adam grabbed me by the shoulders, forcing my attention back to him. His eyes were wide but calm. "All right, gorgeous, I'm more than willing to help you if you're in some kind of trouble here, but ya gotta fill me in. What's going on? Who is that guy?"

I heaved a sigh and dared another peek over my shoulder at the window.

"Holly?"

"Sorry," I said, returning my eyes to Adam's. "Harvey Colepepper is my assigned SPA agent."

"Okay? What's the big deal? We all have one." Adam shrugged.

I shook my head. "This is different. Harvey is different. He doesn't like me."

"Well that much was obvious," Adam said. "What happened between the two of you?"

I sighed. "Remember when I told you that my SPA agent sent me here, to Beechwood Harbor, to keep me out of the reach of my crazy ex-boyfriend?"

Bats, my life sounded like a soap opera.

"That doesn't sound that bad," Adam said, arching an eyebrow.

"Well there's a little more to the story ..."

Adam groaned and rubbed a hand over the back of his neck. "I was afraid of that."

"Harvey found out about my potions business, back when I was living in the Seattle haven. It's technically illegal because it's not registered. I'm not a registered potions master. So *legally* I'm not supposed to be selling potions to other supernaturals."

"Holly ..."

"I know! I know. It's bad. But there was no way the Haven Council was going to grant me my potions master license after everything with Gabriel. I would have been hard-pressed to get one just because of my family name. But then, add in the part about being the ex-girlfriend of an aspiring dark wizard ... you get the picture."

"Okay," Adam held up his hands, his eyes pressed tightly together for a moment. "So, you think he's here to check up on you?"

I peeked past Adam's broad shoulder and stared up at the manor. The light in the new spare bedroom had gone out. A tingle of fear slithered up my spine. "I don't know. But it wouldn't surprise me if he and the rest of the SPA were still investigating me to make sure I haven't had contact with Gabriel."

"Which you haven't, right?"

I frowned at him. "Of course not!"

He held out his palms in surrender. "Okay! Just checking."

I lowered my brows at him. "Bad time to open the ex-files, Adam."

"Noted." He gave a glimmer of a smile. "I know you love your business, Holly, so I'm not going to tell you to close it up, but maybe while your *friend* is in town, you should go on hiatus?"

"I can't, Adam. I have so many orders that I'm barely keeping things in stock. If I take a hiatus now, I'll lose out on all that business and I'll have to explain why. Then no one will buy from me at all."

Adam scratched his jaw. "Is there anywhere else you can work?"

"I don't know. Maybe Evangeline will let me use the spa."

"I'm sure she will. Then you can keep up with production, but we need to come up with another way for you to do your deliveries. We can't have you running around town, toting vials of potions from door-to-supernatural-door. Whether Harvey's here specifically to keep an eye on you or not, he'd probably notice something like that."

I nodded. He was right. I'd have to be even more discreet than usual. I was used to flying under the radar so as to not alert Cassie or any of my other non-magical co-workers at Siren's Song that I was a witch, or that the things that go bump in the night are real and living right under their noses. But Harvey wasn't some blissfully unaware human. He knew what to look for. Especially since he'd caught me once before.

Adam reached out and touched my arm. "We'll figure something out, gorgeous. And hey, worst case scenario, I'll still come visit you in jail."

I narrowed my eyes at him. "Not funny."

Adam's smile faltered. I knew he was only kidding, but the reality of it was still too close to a memory to make light of. I was playing with matches and had just stumbled into a very dry forest. A wildfire was almost inevitable.

CHAPTER 3

*H*arvey stayed in his room for the duration of the night and didn't even come down for dinner. That was probably for the best, since Adam informed me that I was terrible at playing it cool. His exact words were that I should 'leave the acting to Evangeline.' All of my potions were stashed away in the greenhouse, but I remained terrified that one of my customers would knock on the door, or that I'd left some empty vials scattered around and Harvey would pop out from a dark corner, waving them around with a smug little grin. Naturally, every scenario I imagined ended with me being led away in handcuffs.

Thankfully, none of my imaginings came true and the next morning, Evangeline gave me permission to use her supply room as my temporary potion kitchen after I hurriedly explained my dilemma over breakfast. "Of course you can use The Emerald!"

I breathed a sigh of relief. "Thanks, Evangeline. You're a lifesaver."

"Not a problem." She sipped her coffee. "Also, and I'm just tossing this out there, if you ever need help petitioning to the

Haven Council, I have a pretty killer lawyer who could work with you."

"Really?" I'd never considered the option before. After everything with Gabriel and my subsequent banishment, I gave up on the idea of ever getting back into the Seattle haven again, let alone trying to apply for my potions master license.

"Sure." Evangeline set aside her coffee and reached for her fork, digging into the pile of fruit on her plate. "He's not cheap, but he's one of the best in the business and would be willing to take the case if I asked." She paused, her fork poised mid-air, and leaned forward in her seat. "He has a little crush on me," she confessed.

I chuckled and shook my head. "Of course he does."

She smiled and sat back. "Let me know if you want to meet him."

"How much would it cost, do you think?"

She popped a piece of melon into her mouth and gave a little shrug. "Probably low-six figures."

I tried not to choke on my coffee. "What?"

Evangeline cocked her head, as though she couldn't understand my near heart attack.

"That's way out of my price range. I mean, *bats*, Evangeline!"

Her brow furrowed. "You have your royalties from your share of the skin care line at The Emerald, your potion business, and then your salary from Siren's Song on top of that."

"All of which adds up to less than half of what I'd need," I grumbled.

Evangeline's face fell. "Oh."

I sighed. "Is there any way you can sweet talk him into doing some charity work?"

Evangeline laughed softly. "Teddy's not the type to do anything for free. But I'll see what I can do."

"Thanks," I replied, trying to not sound too deflated. It was strange how I felt as though something had been stolen from me, when the option to take my case to the Haven Council wasn't something I'd even considered twenty-four hours ago. But the idea of running my business within the haven system, with the almost limitless potential and reach I would have, was hard to ignore. There was also the bonus of being able to live my life without worrying about the SPA swooping in and carting me off to prison at any given moment.

"The skin care line is going well," Evangeline added conversationally. "I wouldn't be surprised if we sold twice as much next year."

I forced a smile as I gave her a nod, but my stomach twisted into a tight knot. If Harvey found out I was running my potions business, he'd not only shut me down, but Evangeline could potentially get dragged into the crossfire because some of my potions were sold out of her shop. Then she'd need her lawyer friend for her own defense. I hated the idea that I could be putting her in danger. We'd become good friends after initially getting off to an awkward start to our relationship. I didn't want to get her in trouble or risk losing our friendship.

I was about to suggest that maybe we should pull the products until Harvey was out of town again, but I slammed my mouth shut when I heard footsteps on the other side of the kitchen door. Evangeline shot me a look out of the corner of her eye. She'd heard it too. I sat up a little straighter and reached for my coffee mug. Evangeline followed my lead and sipped casually from our mugs like we'd just been discussing the weather.

The door opened and Harvey stalked into the room, his strides clipped and brisk, like he was on a march. He watched

Evangeline and me from the corner of his eye on his way to the fridge. "Good morning, Holly. Evangeline."

Evangeline jerked upright, her eyes going wide with one question: *How does he know who I am?* I narrowed my eyes, remembering that Harvey had known who Adam was the night before without an introduction, either. Was it some kind of SPA magic or was Harvey just downright nosy? I had a feeling I knew the answer to that one.

"Morning, Harvey." I tried to keep my hands from shaking as I stirred a fresh spoonful of cream into my coffee.

Evangeline still looked uncomfortable as she drained the contents of her mug and stood from the table. She snatched her plate and mug up and hurried to deposit them in the sink, carefully skirting around Harvey as he continued to stare at the contents of the fridge. Glancing at me, she said, "I'll see you ... later." She exited the kitchen without even giving me time to respond.

I leveled my stare at Harvey and cleared my throat. "You know the fridge isn't a free-for-all buffet, Harvey. We each pay for our own groceries. No one is going to be happy if you root through everything and take what you want. I'm sure Posy mentioned that on her tour."

She was nothing if not thorough.

Harvey let the fridge door close, revealing that he'd already selected a yogurt cup. "Surely no one will notice if one yogurt goes missing. Besides, this looks like the brand you used to buy, if I'm not mistaken." He popped the top and offered a calculated smile. "I'll pay you back."

My jaw tensed. "I just bet you will ...," I muttered under my breath.

He gestured around the kitchen. "How are things here anyway? Seems you've been keeping your nose clean," he continued, leaning back against the counter. "You'll be happy to know Gabriel is still contained."

I shoved up from the table. "I wasn't worried."

Harvey selected a spoon from the drawer beside him and dug into the yogurt as I dumped my own breakfast dishes in the sink and quickly washed them, along with Evangeline's.

"This home is quite nice. You should be thanking me for sending you someplace so clean and quiet."

I stilled, almost dropping the mug that I was washing. Magic pooled at my palms, sizzling through the dishwater until bubbles rose to the surface. *Keep it together, Holly*, I reminded myself. I took a deep breath and the bubbles disappeared. "I've made the best of it."

He smirked. "I understand you're working at a human shop. What's that like?"

I rolled my eyes and whipped around. "Is this an official SPA interview? Am I under oath here?"

Harvey didn't so much as blink. He took another maddeningly casual bite of his stolen breakfast. "No, just idle conversation. Come now, Holly, I thought we were friends. After all, I saved your skin back in Seattle. If not for me, you'd be sharing the same roof as Gabriel and his misguided friends."

Technically, he was right, but I couldn't shake the feeling that he was fishing for something. Then again, could it be my own guilty conscious telling me to put up a thick wall? If I didn't have anything to hide, would I still feel this hostile? Harvey had kept the SPA from getting their claws into me. Granted, the solution had entailed banishment, but it had all worked out in the end. Hadn't it? If I'd never been banished, I wouldn't have met Posy, Lacey, Nick, Cassie, Evangeline, or any of my other friends in the small town. I certainly wouldn't have met Adam.

I released a heavy sigh. "What are you really doing here, Harvey? Just shoot straight with me. Are you here to check up on me?"

Harvey chuckled and finished off the yogurt. "I assure you, Holly, my arrival in Beechwood Harbor has nothing to do with you." He held up the empty container, flicked it into the air, and I watched as it burst into flames right before my eyes. I frowned as the plastic melted and twisted in mid-air and then popped out of existence. Vanished without a trace. So much for recycling.

Harvey snapped his eyes back to mine. "But, if I find out you're not holding up to your end of the deal, I have no problem taking you back to Seattle when I go."

Without another word, he marched from the kitchen.

∼

HOURS LATER, Harvey's not-so-subtle threat was still echoing around in my mind, making it next to impossible to get any work done. My fingers were clumsy and every chop of my knife seemed to have a voice. *Back to Seattle. Back, back, back* ... After the third attempt at a simple Perky Potion, I extinguished the flame under my kettle and started to pack up the rest of my ingredients.

Evangeline swept into the back room just as I was getting ready to leave. "You're done already?" she asked, turning her back to me to reach for a basket that was perched on the top shelf of the large bookshelf she used to organize her towels and supplies. "I know you're quick, but yeesh."

I waved my hand over the last supplies and they all went to their assigned places inside my small travel potion kit. "I'm not done. I'm giving up," I replied miserably. "At least for today."

Evangeline paused from her rummaging and turned to me, the basket propped on her hip. "Are you all right? Are we being too loud? I tried to get Ben to stop blasting the Christmas music but he just won't listen."

"No. Not at all." I sighed as I leaned forward and braced my hands against the counter. "I just can't focus right now."

Evangeline gave a sage nod. "You're worried about dinner with Adam's parents?"

My eyebrows shot up my forehead. In all the hub-bub with Harvey's arrival, I'd completely forgotten about Adam's parents' looming visit.

Evangeline realized her mistake—likely tipped off by the horrified look on my face—and quickly added, "Not that you have anything to be worried about!"

I plopped into the rolling office chair to the left of the center island and heaved a sigh. "At this rate, I doubt I'll make it to the Yule Feast without getting arrested and thrown into some SPA prison. You met Harvey."

"Yeah. He's ... *intimidating.*"

"That's a good word for him," I replied tiredly.

Evangeline set down her basket. "Holly, you'll be fine. We're not going to let you go to prison. I'll call Teddy and see what he can do to help. In the meantime, you can keep working here as long as you need to, and if I can help with deliveries or anything, just let me know. We're all on your side."

I shook my head. "I can't ask that of you, Evangeline."

"You didn't ask. I'm volunteering."

I cocked my head. "Are you always this stubborn?"

She flashed a wide smile. "Absolutely."

I couldn't help but laugh at her smug expression. She crossed the small storage room and reached out for my hands. I let her heave me up from the chair. "Thank you."

"Anytime. Now, you get back to work, and I'll see what I can do about that Christmas music ..."

I didn't argue as she sauntered from the room, sweeping up her basket of supplies as she went. She pushed the door closed behind her and moments later, I heard her muffled voice as she spoke with Lucy and Ben, warning them that I was not to be disturbed. A few minutes later the music softened and I smiled to myself. It wouldn't hurt to get one more potion done.

My second attempt proved to be much more successful and I started packing up my supplies while the last draught finished simmering. Once the potion was bottled, I stashed it away with the rest of my potion-making kit in the cupboard Evangeline had assigned to me. On my way out of the shop, I noticed that Lacey was there. She and Evangeline were giggling over something in a magazine. I considered joining them, but knew that Adam would be waiting for me back at the manor. I waved to them on my way out and thanked Evangeline for her pep talk.

When I got back to the manor, Adam was sitting at the base of the grand staircase. He was wearing his usual black leather jacket, black t-shirt, and well-worn jeans. A faded navy backpack sat on the step beside him. He must have just taken a shower because his dark hair was still damp and slightly tousled. As I shut the door, he popped to his feet and launched into an explanation before I could ask him what was going on. "I have to go into Seattle," he explained apologetically. "One of my clients got hacked and needs me to come right away."

"Oh no!" I knew that Adam had to go when duty called, but I was still bummed that he had to leave, especially while Harvey was lingering around the manor.

"Sorry, gorgeous. It should only take me a couple of days to get things sorted out." Adam bent to retrieve his backpack and casually draped it over his shoulder. "I'll call you as soon as I get to my hotel for the night."

I nodded and wrapped my arms around myself. My jacket was slick with rain from the quick walk home. "I wish I could go with you," I said miserably.

27

Adam gave me a lopsided smile. "Me, too. But trust me, it won't be any fun. Just a bunch of techy geeks losing their minds cause their bosses are breathing down their necks."

"So that makes you the white knight?"

Adam laughed. "Something like that."

He stepped closer and pulled me into a tight embrace. Adam wasn't really the sentimental type, but he had his moments. I mumbled into his chest, "I'll be fine. I think I'll go back to Evangeline's and hang out with the girls." I glanced over my shoulder, halfway expecting Harvey to pop out from behind a planter. "You know. Keep busy."

Adam gave me a knowing smile. "I think that sounds like a good idea. But you might wanna feed the fur ball first."

I laughed as Boots raced into the foyer, as if on cue. "Sage advice."

Adam pulled the front door open and gave me a quick kiss. "See you soon, gorgeous. Try and stay out of trouble."

"No promises."

He laughed and then stepped across the porch and down the steps.

CHAPTER 4

*T*he following morning, after a quick phone call with Adam, I raced off to work, slipping out the front door before Harvey could ambush me in the kitchen again. Boots wasn't thrilled with my avoidance of the manor, but I assured him it would be a temporary arrangement. At least, I hoped so. Despite the brisk weather, Siren's Song was busy as ever but the foot traffic tended to come in waves, leaving hours with hardly any customers coming through the doors. In the down time, Cassie managed to keep everyone busy with "winter cleaning" which was essentially the same thing as spring cleaning, just three months early.

The project of the day was reorganizing the large cabinets in the supply room, getting rid of everything that hadn't been touched by the fluorescent lights of the shop in the last year. We alternated tasks, serving customers and sorting through the storage containers, until the last cupboards were declared purged of all useless items.

"There," Cassie said, slapping her hands together after shutting the door. "Doesn't that feel better?"

I humored her with a smile. Organizing and cleaning

weren't really my favorite tasks, but it made Cassie happy. "Much," I agreed. "Now, if you ask me, I'd say we've earned a couple of cookies."

Cassie's brilliant blue eyes went wide and she held up a finger. "I have something even better."

"Then by all means, lead the way," I replied, ushering her past me with a dramatic wave of my fingers. She went to the front case and pulled a pale blue box from the bottom shelf. I'd noticed it before, but hadn't stopped to ask what it was. Cassie popped it open, revealing four miniature cakes with small mermaids piped on them. I squealed at the delicate cakes. "Oh my stars! Cassie, these are gorgeous. Where are they from?"

She lifted one of the tiny cakes from the box, spinning it around to inspect it from all angles. "Mrs. Harding took a pastry class and made them for us. Isn't that sweet?"

I swiped at the edge of the cake in Cassie's hand and came away with a dollop of frosting. I popped it into my mouth, savoring the decadent buttercream. "Very sweet," I laughed as Cassie rolled her eyes at the pun.

Cassie handed the cake over. "Guess that one's yours now."

I smiled and took it from her. The mermaids were adorable, but my stomach was growling and the tiny taste of frosting had my mouth watering for more. Without hesitation, I bit a large chunk out of the side. "Mmmm. Did she bake them from scratch? These are Otherworldly!"

Cassie giggled and delicately nibbled at the cake she'd selected. "I'm not sure. If she did, we might have to see about getting in some special orders. Not that Matilda and Penny would be too happy about that."

I flapped a hand. "Don't worry, Adam gives them enough business to keep them rolling along for quite some time."

"I believe it. His appetite is endless. I think every time I see him, he's munching on something. I don't know how he doesn't weigh a ton."

I smiled down at the last bite of cake pinched between my fingers. If only Cassie knew the truth. As a shifter, his energy requirements were off the charts and his constant snacking was just as much a necessity as it was a mindless habit. Cassie had no idea that the large, black dog that ran around town on a weekly basis raiding garbage cans, begging scraps off strangers, and charming the residents of Beechwood Harbor was actually my boyfriend.

"Well, at the moment he's eating his way through the city of Seattle. He left last night to go handle an emergency. Hacking something or another."

Cassie's eyes went round. "Oh, how awful! I hope it's not one of those identity scams. My uncle got caught up in one of those a few months ago. Nasty business."

I gave a sympathetic nod, though I really had no idea what it was or how it worked. The haven system used technology in small doses. Most things ran by magic and magic alone. I didn't know the first thing about hacking and had used a computer less than a dozen times in my entire life. My smart phone and I were constantly at war with one another and besides making calls and texting, I hardly ever used it.

"When will he be back in town?" Cassie asked once she'd polished off the rest of her cake.

"I don't know. I'm supposed to call him when I get home," I replied as I licked the last of the icing off my fingertips.

She consulted the large clock on the wall. "Wow! I can't believe it's almost closing. Time flies when you're having fun!"

I wrinkled my nose. Since when was cleaning and dusting considered *fun*? "Cass, I love you, but you're sick."

She laughed and went to the espresso machine. "You want anything to wash that down?"

I shook my head. "I'm all right."

As she made her drink, I started counting out the tips we'd accumulated throughout the day. They weren't as overwhelming as they'd been over the summer when tourist season was in full swing, but the locals were generous year-round and it had gone up a bit since everyone was in the holiday spirit. As I counted out the money, I wondered how long I would have to make it last. I relied mostly on my potions business to get me by, especially since I cut back my hours at the coffee shop.

I hadn't figured out a way to deliver orders to my customers yet and was still running behind in my production. I was debating asking Evangeline if I could borrow her familiar, Flurry—a tawny hawk—for a few days, but had decided that Harvey would probably notice the large bird swooping from house to house. If I didn't start getting orders out soon, I was going to have to ask Posy if I could get a grace period on my rent.

Cassie finished making her drink and turned to me. "I'm sorry you've had nothing but closing shifts this month. Paisley told me she can start doing some now that she's finished at Thistle."

I shrugged. Right now, the last thing I needed was a reduction in hours. "Don't worry about it. I don't mind closing, especially since I get to see you."

She smiled and bumped me with her hip. "We do make a pretty great team."

"Honestly, I feel guilty not being here to keep you from working yourself into an early grave."

Cassie smiled. "I'm not in danger of that anytime soon. Believe me, Jeffery wouldn't let me anyway."

"How is Chief?" I asked, a mischievous grin taking hold. Cassie had become increasingly secretive about her relationship with the police chief, Jeffery Lincoln, and I had a feeling it was because things were getting more serious than she was ready to talk about just yet.

Cassie's cheeks went pink as she took a longer-than-necessary sip from her coffee. "Things are good. Really good."

I leaned against the counter. "Are you spending Christmas together? You were so nervous about Thanksgiving, but that turned out better than expected, right?"

She nodded. "We haven't talked about Christmas yet, but I know his folks are coming into town."

"Oh?" I arched an eyebrow. "So you're joining my team."

"What team is that?"

"Team awkward."

She laughed softly. "I suppose so. He hasn't asked me to meet them … yet."

"He will," I told her confidently.

Cassie took another lingering sip and as I watched her, I had to ask myself why it was so easy for me to cheer on other people's relationships while I was so terrified of moving forward in my own. After all, Cassie and Chief Lincoln had been dating about the same amount of time as Adam and I had, but from my vantage point, the two relationships couldn't be more different.

Before I could get too tangled up in my musings, Cassie straightened, her gaze sliding to the front doors. I turned to look over my shoulder. "Speak of the devil," I said, right as the little gold bell jangled and Chief Lincoln walked into the shop. Nick, a PI friend of ours, was following close behind, dressed in a pair of black slacks and his dark-grey duster. He must have just finished working.

"Hey, honey," Cassie beamed, smiling from ear to ear at the chief. "I didn't know you were stopping by tonight."

Chief Lincoln lit up brighter than the Christmas tree in

the bay window at the front of the store. "Yeah. The guys kicked me out early."

Cassie's lips twitched. "Were you hovering?"

"Apparently," Chief Lincoln replied with a shrug. "In any case, I figured I'd come see if I could sweet talk you into taking off early, too. I bought a movie and a frozen lasagna."

"Who says romance is dead?" I quipped, glancing at Nick.

He suppressed a smile and leaned against the counter. "Hey—I'm just here for a caffeine fix."

I grabbed a paper cup from the stack by the cash register. "On it."

"Thanks, Holly."

Cassie looked up at the clock above my head. "Would you mind closing up on your own tonight, Holly?"

I took a dramatic glance around the shop, surveying it as though I'd just discovered the Wild West. I could almost see the tumbleweeds rolling. "Gee, Cass, I don't know. It's a little hectic."

She smacked me lightly on the arm as I started making Nick's drink. "I'll take that as a yes." She tugged her apron off and placed it on its proper peg behind the counter, swapping it for her purse and thick winter jacket, which was a vibrant shade of royal purple.

Nick started humming the theme to *Barney*, earning him a fierce glare from both Cassie and Chief Lincoln. I drowned out my own giggle with a blast from the steam wand on the espresso machine.

"See you tomorrow, Holly?" Cassie asked, craning around as Chief Lincoln ushered her to the front door.

"Yup! Have a good night, you crazy kids."

This time I got a scowl from Chief Lincoln, who was a few years older than me.

Nick laughed as the door swung shut behind them. "I still

haven't figured out the key to unlocking Chief's sense of humor. I'm pretty sure it's in there somewhere."

"Must be buried pretty deep," I replied as I passed Nick his mocha and then propped my elbows on the glass pastry case. "What are you up to tonight?"

Nick shrugged and took a sip. "It's pretty miserable out there," he said, glancing over his shoulder to look out the large windows that lined the front of the coffee shop. Nick and I weren't exactly the talk-about-the-weather kind of people, but on a day as gloomy as this one had been, everyone wanted to moan about it. "Chief and Cassie probably have the right idea—warm up some dinner and stay inside with a good movie."

I nodded. "Boots always gets clingy on nights like this, so I'll probably spend it with a tabby attached to my foot while he begs to lick the whipped cream off my hot cocoa. At least he keeps me warm and cozy."

Nick grinned at me. "Is this your subtle way of telling me to get a cat?"

"No." I laughed. "If anything, you need to get a girlfriend."

Nick's smile slid right off his face and, judging by the rapid way he blinked his eyes, I'd caught him completely off guard. The bemused look on his face only made me laugh harder.

"Oh, relax! It was just a suggestion …"

He clasped his hands together in front of him and mumbled something under his breath that I didn't quite catch.

"What was that?" I asked, still grinning.

He gave me a lopsided grin. "Nothing. You should just worry about your big meet-the-parents night before you start issuing relationship advice."

It was my turn to be surprised. "How do you know about that?"

Nick shrugged. "I overheard Evangeline and your other roommate, Lacey, right?" I nodded and he continued, "They were talking about it the other night when I popped in next door," he explained, nodding his head in the direction of the Emerald, which was Siren's Song's only neighbor in the small, circular strip of shops.

"Good to know my love life is such a hot topic," I said with a sigh. "Apparently my roomies are no better than Mrs. Grady and Mrs. Brooks down at the Lucky Lady Salon."

Nick gave me a blank stare.

"Never mind," I arched an eyebrow at him. "What were you doing at The Emerald, anyway?"

His cheeks pinked. "Evangeline's got me hooked on some fancy cream," he grumbled under his breath.

I pressed my lips together to stop another giggle from escaping. The idea of Nick's fancy condo bathroom lined with little pink and green bottles of skin cream painted quite the mental picture.

He frowned at me. "Laugh all you want, the stuff really helps!"

"Whatever you say, Nick," I said, losing the battle to keep myself from laughing.

He glanced around the empty shop, as though looking for some extra masculine task, like chopping wood, or ripping a phone book apart with his bare hands, just to prove his masculinity. Before he could find something, a sing-song chirp sounded from inside his jacket. He fished out his phone and grimaced.

The sound tapered off and he frowned. Seconds later, it rang again and he cursed under his breath.

"Who is it?" I asked as he continued to glare at the phone as though it had personally offended him.

"Georgia Banks."

"Who?"

He held up a finger and took the call. I blinked at the quick change in his demeanor as he plastered on a fake smile, obviously hoping it would transfer to his voice. "Mrs. Banks, how are you?"

Nick paced away from the counter and although I couldn't hear the other side of the conversation, I could tell from the slump of Nick's shoulders that it wasn't going well. Who was this mystery woman who had him so unglued? The name didn't ring any bells and in a small town like Beechwood Harbor, I knew most of the families in the area.

"I understand. Mmhmm." Nick pivoted on his heel and paced back toward the counter. His expression was tight but he still wore the fake smile. The combination made him look slightly deranged. "Yes. I'm on it. I'll call as soon as I know something."

He ended the call and shoved the phone back into the inner pocket of his jacket, muttering to himself.

"What was that little ... *performance?*" I asked, gesturing toward his pocket.

His eyes snapped to me. "What performance?"

I crossed my arms. "You went from 'pissed off' to 'housewife on happy pills' in three seconds flat as soon as you answered your phone. Who is Georgia Banks?"

He groaned and dragged a hand through his short, wavy locks. "My new client. She's from Surfside, lives like her swimming pool is filled with gold coins, and thinks the world revolves around her."

"She has a swimming pool?"

Nick nodded, still scowling.

I tapped my finger against my lips. "I wonder if it actually *is* filled with gold coins."

"Holly," Nick said, frowning at me.

"Right, sorry, sorry. Go on."

"She thinks her husband is working on finding his next

37

wife and wants me to get proof so she can blow up their airtight pre-nup before things go sideways."

I grimaced. "Sounds like fun."

"Yeah. Not so much." He slumped into the nearest chair and stared miserably at his coffee cup. "I might need you to top me off with another double shot before I go. She said her husband left the house, and according to the tracker app she's installed on his phone, he's at some out-of-town motel."

"And she wants you to go into spy mode," I finished, drawing the obvious conclusion.

"That's what pays the bills."

Without another word, I turned to the espresso machine and started pulling another set of shots.

CHAPTER 5

*A*fter topping off Nick's mocha with a couple extra shots of rich espresso, I started breaking down the machine and getting ready to close up for the night. I prepared a bucket of cleanser that sat in the sink and was halfway through attacking the portafilter baskets with an old toothbrush when I realized that Nick was still hovering at the counter. I raised a brow and asked, "Everything okay?"

"I'm waiting for you," he answered before taking another long sip of his drink.

I straightened. "For what?"

"Holly, come on, it's freezing outside. I'm not going to leave and have you walk home. You'd turn into a human Popsicle halfway there."

I smiled at the look of genuine concern on his face. "That's sweet. But I'm fine. I do it all the time. It's not that far."

He frowned. "I'm not taking no for an answer. It's dark and there's already a layer of ice on the sidewalks."

I glanced past his shoulder, out the front window. It wasn't raining, but the air outside would be bitterly cold.

Nights like this had a way of biting through to my skin, regardless of how many layers of clothing I wore. A ride home to the manor in Nick's luxury car didn't sound like a bad idea.

"Well I'm gonna be here for another fifteen minutes. Can you wait that long?"

"Sure." He leaned back in his chair. "Trust me. If Georgia's right about Mr. Bank's whereabouts, then he's not going anywhere anytime soon."

I cringed. "Right."

"Need me to do anything?" He asked, casting a glance around the empty shop. He'd helped me close on a few occasions. I normally put him to work emptying trash cans, but out of boredom during the long afternoon shift, Cassie and I had already taken care of all of the little things.

"I don't think so. I'm going to finish cleaning the machine and then count up the till. Then we can go. But really, Nick, if you need to go—"

Nick flashed a grin. "Holly, come one, you know I'm just as stubborn as you are."

I laughed and went back to work. Nick and I always seemed to be in a battle of wills and I knew firsthand that he wasn't kidding.

Fifteen minutes later, we were bundled into the front seat of Nick's sedan with the heaters on full blast. As Nick pulled out of the Old Town Harbor Shoppes' lot, he glanced over at me. "So, you and Adam got a big movie night planned like Cassie and the chief?"

I shook my head. "Just me and the aforementioned clingy cat tonight. Adam's out of town for a few days."

"Oh?"

"He's in Seattle for some work emergency."

"Hmm. Hopefully nothing too serious." Nick turned onto the main road that led up the hill to the manor. He was taking it slow, babying his expensive car, though from the glistening patches on the road ahead, it was a good decision. He glanced over at me. "So, back at Siren's Song, that crack about the girlfriend—"

"Nick," I said with a laugh. "I was just messing with you. Bats … so touchy."

He chuckled but it felt forced. "Right."

"Why?" I twisted in my seat to face him. "You have your eye on someone? I could work a little *magic*."

Boy, could I! I still had a little of the Fated Flirt potion that I'd whipped up this past summer when I'd been debating dosing him and Cassie. Cassie was with the chief now, but surely there were other eligible candidates in Beechwood Harbor.

"No one specific," Nick replied, keeping his eyes on the road. "I'm a little too busy with work right now anyway. I doubt I'd find someone willing to drop all plans to go on a night time stakeout. Trying to catch someone cheating on their spouse isn't exactly the right backdrop for a romantic night."

"True …" I studied Nick's profile and wondered what was going on inside his head. We'd known each other for several months and he rarely missed his daily trip to the coffee shop, so we saw one another often. On top of that, I'd found that the experience of solving two murder investigations together had a natural bonding quality. However, somehow Nick managed to hold onto an aura of mystery.

I knew the basics, like where he was from, his favorite foods, and that he loved ghost stories and old houses. I even knew about his last girlfriend and the tumultuous ending to that relationship. But I was still foggy on the bigger questions. I had no idea what he really wanted from life. He had a thriving PI business, but was that enough to make him happy? Did he want a wife and kids and a big house up in the hills overlooking the ocean? Or was he content with his shiny condo and the freedom to pick up and move on at a moment's notice?

He caught me staring and arched an eyebrow. "You okay, Holls?"

His voice jolted me back to the present and as my eyes locked with his over the center console, I realized that all of the questions I had about Nick were the same ones I kept asking myself. What did I want? I had my potions business—well, at least until Harvey caught wind and shut me down—and I had Adam. But was that enough? It sure didn't feel like it. There was something hungry and unsatisfied deep inside of me and I hadn't yet figured out what would satiate that beast. Somehow, I had the feeling Nick would understand exactly what I meant if I were to try to explain it.

But I didn't try.

Instead, I flashed an easy smile and asked, "I was just wondering if you'd want some company tonight."

$\approx$

IF MY OFFER SURPRISED NICK, he didn't let on. We stopped at the manor long enough for me to feed Boots and whip up a couple of sandwiches using the leftover spaghetti—the sandwiches were one of Adam's more off-the-wall creations, but darned if they weren't delicious—that I had stashed in the fridge. I grabbed a thicker sweater, a couple of Lemon Clouds, patted Boots on the head, and hurried out again before anyone knew I was home.

We drove to the hotel that Mr. Banks was supposedly staying at for the night and Nick swung his sedan into a parking space with a view of the front entrance. The hotel was part of a national chain and was probably frequented by business people who needed a clean, quiet place to sleep for a night or two. Functional but short on charm. In a word, it was beige—hardly the type of place I'd imagine a torrid affair taking place.

"You sure this is it?" I asked, leaning forward to gaze out Nick's window.

Cassie and Chief's frozen lasagna dinner was more romantic than this place.

"That's what Georgia said." Nick fished his phone from the center console and double-checked the GPS. The robotic voice had spouted directions as he'd driven so it was hard to imagine we had the wrong place. But still …"Yeah. This is it. Stay here, I'm going to go scan the rest of the lot and see if I can spot his car."

I grabbed my messenger-style bag from the floor and started digging around for one of the Lemon Clouds, the magical—and much more delicious—version of a power bar. "Okay. Have fun," I replied as I ripped open a wrapper.

Nick flipped through the phone and spun it around to face me as I stuffed a bite of the decadent pastry into my mouth. "That's our guy. If you see him and he's with someone, try to snap a picture. The camera's right here," he said, popping open the center console. He pulled out a shiny, black camera and handed it to me. "It's pretty simple to work. Point and shoot."

I gave him a mock salute and replied around a mouthful of lemon goodness, "Got it. Point and shoot."

Nick got out of the car and closed the door softly behind him, sealing me in silence. I leaned over and studied the photo still glowing on Nick's phone. Mr. Paul Banks looked normal enough. He was older but appeared to be in good shape based on the cut of his suit. He had salt-and-pepper hair and a clean-shaven face. I used my thumb to flip to the next picture on the roll and found the same man staring at me, this time with his arm wrapped around a busty blonde wearing an incredibly low cut, cobalt-blue evening gown.

"You must be Georgia," I said to the picture. I cocked my head, wondering how on earth she'd managed to keep her dress up. It defied gravity. As I studied their happy faces, I couldn't help but wonder how long ago the photo had been taken. How had they gone from the smiling people in the picture to the state they were in now? Whether Mr. Banks was really cheating or not, it sounded like their happily-ever-after had already come crashing down.

The dark thoughts weren't doing anything to help my already-melancholy mood. I started to swipe to the next picture when I noticed a detail that I'd overlooked at first because I was distracted by the sheer amount of skin on display—around Georgia's neck hung a gold medallion. Using my finger and thumb, I zoomed into the picture and studied the face of the round piece of jewelry.

Etched into the gold was a symbol I'd seen many times, but never outside of a haven. The Thraxis was a mythical three-winged bird, depicted wearing a stately crown, and was a symbol adopted by the Molder House—a *very* old and powerful family of vampires. What was Georgia doing with a necklace like that? My pulse quickened as a flurry of questions started bouncing around my in head like popping corn: Was she a vampire? Was Paul? If so, did either of the other know? Or maybe they were *both* vampires ...

Whatever the case, the Thraxis' sudden appearance made whatever was going on feel a lot more dangerous. Warring vampire situations—even in the case of a husband and wife—could turn volatile in a hurry, as most vamps were severely lacking in the impulse-control department. I made a mental note to ask Nick if he'd ever met Georgia outside, in broad daylight.

True to classic folklore, vampires couldn't go out into the

sun. And no, it wasn't for fear of *sparkling*. Most of them, within a few minutes of exposure, would develop a severe skin rash that was like an intense sunburn. On cloudy days, with the right amount of protective clothing, they could go out and about during daylight hours, but most of them preferred to stick with the whole *creatures of the night* thing.

My heart sputtered into a frantic beat as I scanned the dark parking lot. If Paul *was* a vampire, he wouldn't take too kindly to Nick stalking him and would have the advantage of being able to pick up on Nick's presence long before Nick realized he was being watched. And if he felt threatened …

There was no telling what he might do.

I tossed the phone down on the driver's seat and scrambled to get out of the car. I couldn't risk the chance that Paul would pick Nick up on his radar. Not if Paul was what I thought he might be. As I started around the hood of the car, I racked my brain, trying to remember the names of the most prominent figures in the Molder family. I wasn't as familiar with the vampire houses as I should have been, considering quite a few of them called the Seattle haven home. It was the perfect city for vampires thanks to the lack of sunlight and general gloom nine months out of the year. *Paul* Molder didn't ring any bells but that didn't mean there wasn't a link to the family. For all I knew, Paul Banks was a fake name.

Halfway across the lot, toward the front of the hotel, I spotted him. Paul Banks was indeed at the hotel—and accompanied by a lanky brunette. My eyes narrowed as I tried to get a better look. If Paul was a vampire—a Molder, no less—then there was the distinct possibility that he wasn't cheating on his soon-to-be-ex-wife, but instead … preparing for his next *meal*.

Paul stroked a finger down the side of the brunette's face as she gazed adoringly up at him. His finger slipped past her jaw and traced the lines on her throat. I gulped loudly, trying to push my heart out of my throat. All I knew was that Nick and I needed to get out of there before the parking lot turned into an all-you-can-eat buffet.

I whirled around, looking for Nick. Suddenly, somebody grabbed my wrist and yanked me to the ground with a sharp tug.

CHAPTER 6

I caught myself before I hit the pavement. Magic sparked to life in the palm of my hand, a stunning spell at the ready as I twisted around to see who had a hold of my arm. "Let me—"

"Holly!" Nick hissed, his eyes wide. He placed a finger over his lips, silently shushing me, then made a grabbing gesture. I furrowed my brows at him and he whispered, "Camera?"

Bats! "I didn't bring it," I whispered back.

He gave me a strange look, like he was trying to figure out what was wrong with me. "Then what are you doing out here?" he asked, still keeping his voice low.

I licked my lips and glanced back in the direction of Paul and his leggy date/possible dinner. "I—uh—"

Nick didn't wait for me to come up with an answer and jogged back to his car. I stayed crouched down behind the cement barricade that encircled the parking lot and peeked back over the top. The brunette was clinging to Paul like he was a life raft. Her full lips curved into a flirtatious smile as Paul whispered something in her ear.

He dropped his lips lower and my heart jumped into my throat. "Not on my watch, pal," I muttered. I rubbed my fingers together, conjuring a stunning spell so powerful the magic hummed against my own skin. I glanced over my shoulder. Nick was bent over, half his torso inside the car as he reached for the camera. I didn't have time to waste. I turned back and raised my hand, ready to strike.

Paul and his mystery woman were gone.

I blinked, wondering if I'd somehow imagined the whole thing. They couldn't have just *vanished*. Could they? The hotel door flapped shut and I cringed. "Bats!" Nick was going to kill me. Worse than that, I might have missed my one chance to save the brunette from a grizzly end. I'd become accustomed to tame vampires—civilized undead creatures that coexisted with other supernaturals, and even humans, without issue. However, the Molder family was one of the oldest vampire families in existence, and if gossip was to be believed, there were pockets of members that believed in the so-called "ancient" ways. I didn't know if Paul Banks was one of them—or if he was even a vampire—but if something happened to the woman and I could have stopped it, I'd never be able to forgive myself.

"Where did they go?" Nick asked, crouching back beside me.

I jumped and slapped my hands together to smother the magic that lingered there. "I think they just went inside," I said, jutting my chin in the direction of the front doors. "Can we go in after them? Pretend to be guests?"

Nick sighed impatiently. I could feel a lecture coming on, but before he could launch into it, the couple reappeared. "Wait," I hissed. I jerked on the sleeve of his jacket and pointed across the lot as Paul and the brunette stepped out of the shadows. They hadn't gone inside after all. From the disheveled appearance of her short dress, they'd been over-come by the heat of the moment …

Nick raised the camera over the cement barrier and snapped a series of rapid-fire pictures. The couple was so lost in each other that they didn't even notice the soft clicking sounds. Paul removed his hands from the woman long enough to open the hotel's front doors and ushered her inside, stopping just long enough to steal another kiss on the way.

"Bingo," Nick whispered, snapping another shot at the exact right moment. "That's what we call the money shot."

I frowned over at him. "I thought you didn't like catching cheating spouses."

"I don't," he agreed, lowering the camera. "But I will enjoy collecting a fat check from Mrs. Banks *and* being rid of her hour-long phone calls."

"Hour-long calls?" I asked incredulously.

"Yeah," he replied wryly. "I'm starting to feel like I got into the wrong business. Half the time, I'm playing psychologist anyway …" He muttered something else under his breath as he pushed up from his squatting position. I glanced back at the hotel's entrance and racked my brain for a reason to stay and wait a little longer. Nick had what he needed and I should get back to the manor. It was dark and freezing, and from the feeling in the air, rain wasn't too far off. But I couldn't ignore the churning in my gut as I wondered what would happen once Paul got the woman behind closed doors.

"You ready?" Nick asked.

I tore my eyes from the hotel and saw that he'd already started back for the car. "Yeah. I was just … thinking."

"I can see that." He gave me a soft smile and waited for me to catch up before continuing to the car. "What's on your mind?"

I sighed, unsure how to explain the heavy feeling in my gut without revealing why I had it. I couldn't tell Nick anything about my suspicions or the necklace that Georgia was wearing in the picture on his phone. Nick wasn't from my world and there was no way I could bring him into it, even if it would make things a whole heck of a lot easier sometimes.

He paused before opening the driver's side door and considered me from across the roof of the sedan. A sudden look of realization crossed his face. "Jeez, I feel like such an idiot. You've been cheated on before, haven't you?"

My eyebrows went sky high. "What?"

"Your ex? Did he ever cheat on you? Is that what you're thinking about?"

"No. Gabriel wasn't a cheater." I shook my head. "Or at least, not in that way." I tugged the car door open and dropped into the passenger seat. Nick slid into the driver's seat and we buckled up, carefully avoiding eye contact.

Nick fiddled with his keys. "Sorry, Holly. I shouldn't have even asked. That's obviously none of my business."

I glanced over at him and tried to reassure him with a faint smile. "It's fine, Nick. Don't worry about it."

He nodded but then let out a heavy sigh. He dropped his head back and stared up at the ceiling for a long moment. "These cases get to me, Holls. I didn't mean to make light of it."

I briefly met his gaze and instantly wished I hadn't. His normally bright blue eyes were dark in the low lighting and had a deep, intense quality to them that I hadn't seen before. There was something magnetic and arresting about the way he looked and I couldn't blink. Or breathe.

"It's sad," he continued. "When stuff like this happens. You gotta figure that at some point, Paul and Georgia Banks were this crazy, hopelessly-in-love couple. They had plans and dreams for their future. And now ... six years later ... they're ready to go their separate ways and all those good years may as well never have even happened."

I swallowed hard. "Some things just aren't meant to last."

"I guess not."

Nick broke eye contact first and my heart sputtered back into action. He looked out the driver's side window, back at the hotel entrance.

"Now what?" I asked after a long moment.

Nick hitched a single shoulder. "We leave. I'll send the photos to Georgia in the morning and let her do with them whatever she pleases."

I bobbed my head and interlaced my fingers together in my lap. "Right."

"You sure you're okay, Holly?"

"I'm sure," I answered, wishing for the dozenth time that I could simply tell him the truth. About everything. If there was one person who would understand—even welcome—the supernatural world I lived in, it was Nick. But I couldn't. It would be too big of a risk, especially when I was already on thin ice with Harvey and the SPA.

"All right. Let's get out of this weather then," Nick said as he turned the key in the ignition. The car purred to life and a blast of hot air streamed almost instantly from the vents. Without another word, he pulled out of the compact parking space and headed back toward the road. We remained lost in our own thoughts as he drove back into Beechwood Harbor. My mind bounced all over the place, jumping from the past, to the present, to the future, and then back again, coming up with more questions but finding no answers.

Nick pulled up along the sidewalk in front of the manor and we both stared up at the stately home. The porch lights were on, illuminating the immaculately maintained facade. Several interior lights were lit and I spotted Boots' silhouette jumping down from one of the second-level sills, likely getting ready to charge me the moment I stepped inside. I smiled to myself and reached for the door handle, but then paused. It felt like there was something that needed to be said, but I wasn't sure what it was.

In the end, Nick broke the silence first as he twisted in his seat and smiled at me. "Thanks for coming with me tonight, Holly. It was nice to have some company for once."

I slung my purse over my shoulder. "Sure thing. It's fun to play super spy sometimes."

"You might need to log a few more hours to launch yourself into the *super* category, but you're getting there." Nick's eyes danced in the soft light of the cab. Suddenly it was like I couldn't quite take a full breath, as though the air were thinning. I flailed to open the door, my fingers missing the handle on the first attempt. "Here," he said, leaning across to unlatch the door. "Goodnight, Holly."

"Night, Nick."

I hurried to untangle myself from the seat belt and then started up the walk. I paused at the front porch to look over my shoulder and watch Nick drive away. A dull ache in my chest refused to leave and I knew it had nothing to do with the fact that somewhere across town, a dangerous vampire might be on the loose.

I heaved a sigh and tried to put the whole strange evening out of my mind as I entered the manor. After all, I'd been under a lot of stress lately.

After a fitful night of sleep, I woke up still feeling out of sorts, and things only got worse when I arrived at Siren's Song. Nick burst through the doors before I could even finish tying my apron around my waist, and his face was so pale that he could have given Lacey a run for her money. He rushed to the counter, and as he placed his hands on the smooth Formica, I noticed they were shaking.

"Nick? What's wrong?"

He leaned over the desk, his eyes wild. "You remember Mr. Banks, from last night?"

I nodded, my brows knitting together. "Yeah? What about him?"

"Holly." Nick drew in a deep breath. "He's dead."

CHAPTER 7

"*D*ead?" I repeated, desperately hoping I'd misheard Nick's proclamation.

To my horror, he nodded. "They found him this morning, in that same hotel room."

"Bats …" I glanced around, assuring myself that no one was listening. "What—uh—what happened?"

"He was found by the maid, dead in the bathtub."

"The bathtub? What are we talking, toaster in the tub? Or—"

"I don't think so." Nick shook his head. "I don't know much at this point. I heard the call over the scanner and recognized the address. When I got there, the team was still working the scene and I wasn't able to go in."

As a private investigator and former journalist, Nick was adept at keeping his finger on the pulse of the news items in the small community. It wasn't a secret that he had access to a couple of police scanners and listened to them like some people would listen to a radio station. He claimed it was an old habit. Since his arrival in Beechwood Harbor, he had established quite the rapport with Chief Lincoln, but he still wasn't able to have free reign over crime scenes or get unlimited access to police files. The details of the case would leak out over the following days.

I swallowed the lump in my throat. "What about his, uh, date?"

Nick ducked his chin. "No one knows where she is but she wasn't in the hotel room. So either she'd already left by the time he was attacked, or whoever killed him took her with them."

"So, she might have gotten away? Made a run for it?"

Nick considered the theory and nodded. "It's possible. I'll know more when I get a chance to talk to Chief Lincoln. He wants to see me at the station in an hour to go over my statement. I already gave him a description of the woman so they can try to find out who she is." Nick paused for a few seconds. "Or, it's possible she's the one who did it."

I turned the theory over in my head. She wouldn't have been able to escape Paul if he were a vampire. At least, the odds were low. But if he wasn't? Maybe they'd had a fight? A lovers' quarrel gone too far? It was horrifying either way, but I would rest somewhat easier knowing vampires weren't tangled up in the murder.

A new, even more somber thought popped into my head. "How's Georgia taking it?" I asked, almost afraid of the answer.

Nick frowned. "She hasn't answered her phone. I don't even know if she knows yet."

My stomach turned. "That's awful."

Nick shifted uncomfortably. "I suppose it's not really news that should be delivered over the phone anyway. Chief Lincoln is headed over to speak with her."

The room took on a sudden chill. I folded my arms and rubbed my biceps with my hands. Whatever their differences were, he had still been her husband. I couldn't imagine what it would be like to get that kind of news. "Are you going to show her the pictures?"

With a pained expression, Nick nodded. "I have to see if she knows the woman he was with. The police need that ID. The more information they can get, the faster they can track down whoever did this."

"Is there anything I can do to help?"

"Chief Lincoln will probably want to get your statement from last night. I told him you were with me when I got the pictures of Paul."

"Right." I made a move toward the espresso machine. "You need a coffee for the ride?"

Nick shook his head. "I don't think I could stomach anything right now. I'll stop by later though, okay?"

"Okay." I rested a hand on the counter. "Tell Chief Lincoln I'll be here all day if he needs me."

"Will do." Nick backed up and exited the shop just as the first push of the morning rush was on the way in.

Cassie emerged from the back room at the sound of the bell ringing. She joined me at the counter as the cluster of peopled formed a line. "Was that Nick?"

I nodded, still dazed.

"Holly? You okay?"

I jumped at her feather-light touch on my shoulder. "What? Oh, yeah, I'm fine. You wanna take orders or do drinks?"

"I'll work the bar," she said, sliding into place at the espresso machine. She launched into whipping up orders made from memory, as most of the people lining up at the register were regulars who rarely strayed from their normal orders.

I plastered a smile on my face, shoving aside the thoughts of vampires, murdered husbands, and the sad, lost look in

Nick's eyes, and concentrated on getting through the day without having a breakdown.

~

BY THE TIME I got back to the manor after a long, ten-hour shift, I was mentally and physically exhausted. My feet ached and my stomach was churning, practically begging me for something more substantial than the three sugar cookies and large coffee I'd had for lunch. The manor was quiet when I stepped inside, but as soon as I closed the door behind me, I heard the sound of frantic paws on the floor. Boots crashed against me half a heartbeat later.

"It's nice to know you'll always be here, ready to greet me," I told him, stooping over to scratch at his favorite spot under his chin.

As much as I liked spending time with Adam in the evenings, I had to admit there was something nice about coming home to a quiet house every now and then. Especially after a long day. I didn't have to worry about getting right back into my coat to go down to McNally's for dinner. Then again, at least with Adam around, there was always good food. As it was, I'd probably crack open a can of soup and call it good enough.

My stomach rumbled loudly and I started to the kitchen, following Boots, who was, predictably, just as eager for dinner. I popped the top on a can of cat food before opening a can of soup for myself. "This is some pretty high class dining here, Bootsie," I said sarcastically, frowning at the gloppy mess inside the soup can.

He was too busy inhaling his own dinner to commiserate.

A flick of my fingers had a fire crackling under the large green kettle on the stove. I supposed I should get out a proper saucepan, but the kettle was infinitely more convenient and I was feeling too lazy to put in much more effort. While the contents simmered, I pulled my phone from the pocket of my jeans and checked through my messages. Adam had texted earlier in the afternoon, asking me to call him when I was back home, so I dialed his number and propped the phone against my shoulder while I finished heating up my dinner.

He answered on the third ring. "Hey, gorgeous." He sounded tired but the hint of a smile warmed my heart and I found myself missing him. As much as I'd wanted the peace and quiet, I suddenly wanted the chaos and noise: Adam and Lacey taking shots at each other, Posy trying to break up the argument, Evangeline peppering me with questions about a new potion she wanted to attempt.

"Hey stranger," I replied with a wistful smile as I removed my simmering soup from the heat. "How was the day?"

Adam answered my question by rattling off some string of words that all sounded like English, but with the amount of techy mumbo-gumbo mixed it, it may as well have been Swahili.

I laughed softly. "So … good?"

Adam chuckled. "Making progress."

I poured the soup into a deep ceramic bowl, grabbed a sleeve of crackers from Adam's snack cupboard, and made my way to the table. "How much longer are you going to be in Seattle?"

Adam heaved a sigh. "At least another day. They want me to double—and then triple—check the security to make sure this can't happen again."

"All right. Well try to hurry back," I said.

"You getting lonely over there?" he asked flirtatiously. I pictured his face, the half-cocked smile he was sure to be wearing, and missed him all over again.

I threw on my best Scarlet O'Hara voice and said, "Oh,

desperately! I do declare, I don't know what to do with myself without you by my side."

Adam laughed. "You're impossible."

"Just answer one question. What do you miss more? Me or the bakery?"

"Hmm. That's a tough one—"

"Adam!"

"Come on, gorgeous," he said, laughing. "That's easy. Obviously, I miss Boots the most."

I rolled my eyes and lounged back in my chair. "Who is this? And what have you done with my boyfriend?"

"He'll be fine. You can have him back in exchange for two cinnamon rolls with extra frosting."

I laughed under my breath. "That sounds more like the Adam I know."

He joined in my easy laughter and I relaxed against the chair. "You know I miss you like crazy."

"But you still want the cinnamon rolls," I quipped.

"Well …"

"Listen, there's actually something I wanted to ask you," I said, leaning forward. I propped my elbows on the edge of the table and twirled my spoon through my rapidly cooling soup. "Off the topic of pastries."

Adam chuckled and then replied, "Fire when ready."

"What do you know about the Molder family?"

"Vamps?"

"Yeah."

He sighed and asked warily, "Why?"

I frowned into my soup. He really wasn't going to like the second part of my question. "Let's just say, hypothetically of course, that I may need to know exactly what they're capable of in case I need to talk to a few of them."

"And *why* would you need to talk to them?" Adam asked, his irritation rising.

"I said it was hypothetical."

"Holly …"

I squeezed my eyes closed and rattled off the facts as though the speed of delivery would somehow soften the blow. "Because I think Nick's client might be one—or was married to one—till he ended up dead in a hotel-room bathtub. Oh, and the woman he was last seen with has gone missing."

At the end of my explanation, Adam groaned. "Holly …"

"I know, I know. Trust me, I don't go looking for these situations. I just always seem to land in the middle of them." I really needed to figure out why that was. "But Adam, if this is really something to do with the Molder family, I can't just let Nick figure it out on his own. He's no match for any of them, and you know it. I know you and Nick have your differences, but you don't want him to end up getting taken down by some vampire on a binge."

A long moment of silence stretched out between us.

"Adam?"

"Okay, okay. Fine," he growled. "But Holly, you have to promise me that you'll stay far away from the Molders. You might think you have an inkling as to how dangerous they are, but I can assure you, the stories you've heard are not only true, but just the tip of the iceberg. If you don't believe me, just ask Lacey."

I glanced up at the ceiling and trained my eyes in the general direction of Lacey's room. She was likely already out of the house for the night but I made a mental note to corner her as soon as she got back. "I promise I won't go looking for trouble. But I have to keep Nick safe."

Adam didn't say anything, but his silence relayed his disapproval loud and clear.

The rest of the conversation was tense, and no matter how I tried to wiggle back into his good graces, I wasn't able to recapture the ease and flirtation it started with. After a few more false starts, we wrapped up the call and said goodnight. I ended the call and set it on the table beside my bowl of soup, then glanced down at Boots. "Be thankful you're a cat, Bootsie."

CHAPTER 8

A knock on the front door interrupted my miserable dinner as I sulked over my bowl of soup, regretting the frosty conversation with Adam. Boots was asleep on the tufted cat bed by the back door and didn't raise his head at the sound. The manor was still quiet and after the second knock, I decided that I was home alone. I could normally count on Posy to float through the kitchen wall and tell me who was out on the porch waiting to be let in, but even she was absent. I shoved up from my place at the table, abandoned my now-cold soup, and went to answer the door.

Chief Lincoln was waiting on the front steps. He was dressed casually in a pair of dark jeans and a puffy waterproof coat. He reached up and tipped the bill of his ball cap. "Evening, Holly."

"Hello, Chief." I glanced behind me, unsure if I should let him in. The coast still looked clear and without Adam around to provoke Lacey, things would likely remain quiet. As long as Harvey didn't come wandering through, we should be safe. Harvey, unlike the rest of my supernatural roomies, would be harder to explain. Lacey could hide her fangs, Evangeline could keep her magic wand stowed out of sight, and humans couldn't see Posy, but a three-and-a-half-foot-tall goblin-hybrid with sharp teeth and a grouchy disposition would be harder to explain away. "Did you want to come inside?" I asked, turning back to face him. It wasn't the kind of night for a talk on the front porch. While the rain had stopped, it was still bitterly cold and a wind was whipping through the trees that enclosed the property.

Chief Lincoln nodded and I took a step back to allow him entrance. "Thank you."

"We can go into the sitting room."

He nodded and then followed my lead. "I take it you already know what this visit is in regards to."

We entered the sitting room and I waited for him to sit down on the loveseat before I took my place on the couch. I nodded. "Nick came by the shop today. He told me you had some questions for me."

"Okay. Good." Chief Lincoln unzipped his jacket and dug out the small moleskin notebook he always had on him. I'd once asked Cassie if he took it to bed with him. She'd gone a splendid shade of maroon and ignored the question.

"He didn't give me any details," I hurried to add. The last thing I wanted to do was get Nick in trouble. "Just that Mr. Banks was found dead and that the woman we saw him with was nowhere to be found."

Chief Lincoln flipped to a fresh page. "Well, as you likely know, I can't provide much more information than what you already know. It's an open investigation but there's no question that this was a murder. As such, I need to get your official statement as to what you saw last night."

I laced my fingers together and anchored them in my lap to keep them from twitching. "Nick was taking me home from work and got the call from his client, Mrs. Banks, and I volunteered to go with him to the hotel—"

"And how is it that Mr. Rivers knew where the victim would be?"

I blinked, assuming Nick had already provided that detail. "Um, Georgia—Mrs. Banks—gave him the address. I think she texted it to him and he put it into the GPS."

Chief Lincoln rolled his fingers through the air. "Right, but where did *she* get that information?"

I swallowed hard. "Nick said she put an app on his phone. It tracked him. She thought he was cheating on her and she wanted to get proof. Something about breaking a pre-nup. It sounded *messy*."

Chief Lincoln didn't say anything as he continued to scribble notes down. "Go on. What happened when you got to the hotel?"

I shifted in my seat. It was time to downplay the entire scene. "Mr. Banks was there, in the parking lot, with a brunette. I don't know who she was, but it was definitely not Mrs. Banks."

"How did they seem?"

I shrugged a shoulder. "Happy. Carefree. Passionate. If I'd just seen them, and didn't know the background, I would have thought they were a long-term couple."

Chief Lincoln glanced up from his note-taking. "Did you overhear any of their conversation?

"No." I shook my head. "To be blunt, Chief, it didn't look like they were there to talk if you know what I mean." My cheeks warmed. I didn't want to fill in the blanks. Detailing how the victims were philandering in the shadows of the hotel wasn't exactly a play-by-play I wanted to give to Chief Lincoln.

"Right." He leaned forward, as though preparing to push up from his seat. "And after they went inside, you didn't see anything else? Anyone else in the lot or going into the hotel?"

"No. Well—"

"What?"

"When Nick was getting the camera, I thought they'd gone inside. The door was swinging shut like someone had just gone in. But then they came out from the shadows along the side of the hotel. So someone else must have gone in. Or out, I suppose. But I didn't see them."

Chief Lincoln frowned. "We're pulling the security footage so if someone else was there, we'll find out."

I nodded. "Smart. Do you think this was a random attack?"

Chief Lincoln set his pen down in the binding of his notebook. "We're not sure. It has a personal feel to it. A crime of passion, if you will."

"So you think it was the woman he was with?"

"Honestly? Considering the nature of the attack, I would be surprised if it was a woman. There was a struggle. A nasty one, from what we can gather. Judging by the photographs Nick provided, Paul Banks had a good fifty pounds on his date and at least three inches."

"Probably more," I interjected. Chief Lincoln raised his brows and I shrugged sheepishly. "She was wearing killer heels. I have a thing for shoes."

He picked up his pen and took down another note. "In any case, unless she had some kind of adrenaline-fueled moment of super strength, I don't think she could have held her own in a physical fight with the victim and managed to do as much damage as the murderer did."

I shuddered. I didn't want to dwell on the crime scene, especially if my suspicion about vampires being involved was true. After all, they have a thing for blood.

"Is there anything else that you think might help?"

I considered his question and then shook my head. "Not really. Nick took some pictures before they went inside. It was cold and getting late. So he drove me home, dropped me off here, and that was it."

Chief Lincoln wedged his pen between the notebook's pages and tucked it back into his jacket's interior pocket. He zipped his jacket up to the neck and offered a polite smile. "Thank you, Holly. By now you know the drill. If I have any other questions—"

"You'll let me know."

He smiled and gave me a nod. "That's right."

We stood and I escorted him back to the front door. A blast of cold air greeted us as I opened the door and Chief Lincoln frowned as he looked out into the night.

"You all right, Chief?"

He hesitated for a moment before bringing his gaze back to mine. "It's just been a long day, that's all." Something about the way he said it made me think there was more going on inside his head. I paused, not sure if it was my place to pry. He was dating my best friend, but he also struck me as an extremely private person and a man of few words. After another long moment, he sighed. "I've never seen anything like the crime scene today. It was something out of a horror movie, Holly. These things aren't supposed to happen here in Beechwood Harbor or our neighboring communities."

I nodded, agreeing with his grim assessment. "Trust me, Chief, this isn't exactly what I signed up for when I moved here either."

A slight smile tugged at his lips. "I'll bet."

"It's a good thing we have good cops, like you and your deputies. I know you'll find out who did this and make sure that justice is served."

"Thank you, Holly." The emotion in his eyes almost startled me. I'd never seen him look so raw. Whatever had been waiting on the other side of that hotel room's door had rattled him. Big time.

The realization sank deep into the pit of my stomach and ignited the urgency to figure out who was behind the attack and why. Chief Lincoln was a good cop—and an excellent shot as I'd learned months before—but if the Molder family was involved, he wouldn't stand a chance.

"Goodnight, Holly. Thank you for your time."

"Anytime, Chief. Let me know if there is anything else I can do to help."

He looked ready to argue, to give me the same speech he'd given me on two other occasions—stay out of it—but at the last moment, he appeared to have a change of heart and swallowed the warning. He smiled, tipped his hat, and left the manor.

I watched as he walked down the path leading to the sidewalk where his unmarked car was parked. Once he was behind the wheel, I shut the front door and dragged in a deep breath. The people of Beechwood Harbor had all become like family to me and I would go to the Otherworld and back if that's what it took to keep them all safe. Despite Adam's warnings and worrying, despite the danger, and likely despite my own better judgment, I wasn't going to stand by and let anyone I loved get hurt.

"What was that about?"

My heart leapt into my throat at the sound of Harvey's gravelly voice and I whipped around to find him standing at the base of the staircase. His arms were crossed and his beady eyes were narrowed in my direction, giving him a menacing look. I wrapped my own arms around myself and returned his harsh glare. "Spying on me now?"

Harvey didn't so much as blink. "Why was the police chief here?"

I didn't even waste my breath asking how he knew who Chief Lincoln was. "It's none of your business, Harvey. It's a town matter."

I considered asking him what he knew about the Molder family, and briefly wondered if they had anything to do with his arrival in town. But before I could ask, he snapped his fingers and vanished right in front of my eyes.

I stared, open-mouthed, at the place he'd just stood. "I did *not* know he could do that," I said to the empty room.

CHAPTER 9

The following morning I wandered into town and made my way to Siren's Song even though I wasn't on the schedule. I needed a caffeine fix and a pastry the size of my head. Siren's Song could provide both, and a visit would give me an excuse to hang around, listen to the town gossip, and see if anyone had anything to say that might be helpful. Surely by now, everyone knew that a grisly murder had been committed just outside of town, and there was no doubt that everyone would have an opinion and half-cocked theory. If I was lucky, some of the chit-chat might prove to be valuable.

Cassie turned to greet me as I stumbled inside. "Morning, Holly."

"Morning." I shuffled to the counter. "Coffee. Bear claw. Stat."

"Perfecting your Walking Dead audition?" She stifled a laugh and picked up a pair of tongs to snag a pastry from the front case. "You'd think you would be more of a morning person. You've been working here for almost a year now."

I shrugged. "My body rebels and goes back to its true nature on my days off."

She handed the pastry over and then went to work pouring a large coffee. "What's on your agenda for the day?" she asked. Cassie didn't know about my side business and when I'd asked to cut back my hours at the coffee shop, I'd had to convince her that I was taking some online classes, which was only half a lie. I'd been studying potion work and spending more time with textbooks and ancient scrolls than I had since my academy days.

"Not too much today," I replied. I cast a glance around the shop and frowned as I realized there were only three other customers in the seating area. All of them were wearing earbuds and didn't look like they were likely to launch into a lively discussion of a recent murder case anytime soon. The Lucky Lady Salon would be the place to go for fresh gossip. All the older, retired ladies in Beechwood Harbor liked to gather there and they always had the best dirt. But it would take hours to glean anything useful, and I'd have to endure their nosing and prodding about my relationship with Adam. No, it would be best to have Posy flag down Gwen later and get the scoop. Gwen was a permanent fixture at the salon and would be able to give me the rundown. Ghosts really had it easy—endless eavesdropping and the freedom to leave at any time, without the pressure of making up an excuse when the conversation got boring.

"If you want, you could come over tonight after we close. Kirra, Paisley, and I are doing a movie and manicure night." Cassie set my coffee in front of me. "Jeffery's working some big case and had to cancel our normal date, so I've declared it girl's night."

"Sounds fun. I'll have to see what's going on with Adam. He's supposed to be coming home. Hopefully tonight."

"Oh, yeah!" Cassie's sapphire eyes sparkled. She found the

entire predicament way too amusing. "When are his parents coming into town?"

I groaned. "I still have a week."

"You think you're getting something sparkly under the tree this year?" she asked, wiggling her ring-finger in my direction.

I rolled my eyes. "No, Cass. I don't."

She frowned at me and dropped her hand to the counter with an unceremonious *plop*. "Why not?"

I quirked my lips to one side. "Are *you* expecting something sparkly under the tree this year?"

Her smile faltered. "No."

"Oh? And why not?" I asked, mimicking her sing-song tone.

Cassie sighed and gave me an irritated look. "You wreck all my fun."

"Sorry, doll. But, remember, these questions and teasing can always be turned right around. You two have been together nearly as long as Adam and I have." I winked at her, thanked her for the coffee, and headed for the front door. "I'll call you later about girl's night. Maybe Evangeline would want to tag along."

"You could invite Lacey, too," she said.

I smirked down at my coffee. "Oh, yeah, she'd love that."

"Let me know. Enjoy your free day!"

"Thanks, Cassie. I'll call you later." I waved and headed back out into the cold. The warmth from the cup of coffee in my hands seeped through my thin gloves and provided a tiny bit of comfort as I paused outside, mentally debating where to go. Curiosity called to me and led me off the path back to the manor, taking me across the street and down a few blocks to the historic building where Nick rented an office space. His office was at the end of hall and as I neared, I saw his light was on, shining through the frosted glass window. "Workaholic," I said, shaking my head. "At least he's predictable."

I tapped lightly on the door as I opened it to peek inside. Nick looked up from his place behind his large desk. He looked like he hadn't slept since getting the news about the murder. Deep lines were etched around his eyes and the startling blue color had been replaced by a lackluster grey.

"Hey," I said, venturing further into the office. The door slid closed behind me and latched with a soft click. I took one of the navy blue chairs opposite him and crossed my ankles. "I'm just gonna say it: you look like something the cat dragged in. Not that I'm an expert—Boots is far too lazy for such excursions."

I hoped for a smile but had to settle for a slight twitch of his lips. "I had a meeting with Georgia this morning."

I dropped my eyes to my feet. "Oh."

Nick sighed heavily. "Yeah."

I met his exhausted eyes. "I'm sorry, Nick. That's gotta be the worst part of this job."

He gave a slight nod. "Chief Lincoln had already broken the news to her, but obviously she was just as raw when I arrived a couple of hours later."

"So, she knows that Paul was … not alone … that night?"

"I showed her the pictures. I didn't want to but she insisted." Nick steepled his fingers together and braced his elbows on the edge of the desk. "She doesn't know who the woman is. She said she's never seen her before and in all her spying on Paul, she'd never come across any proof of a stable relationship. She just figured he was picking up random women in bars."

"So the woman could be someone he just met?"

Nick nodded. "It's possible. The hotel doesn't have her name on file. Paul didn't even have a reservation. It seems like it was a last minute decision. As far as I can tell, he and

Georgia got into an argument, he left to go get a drink, and when he didn't come home, Georgia logged into the app and saw his phone registering at the hotel."

"Makes sense. Chief Lincoln came to the manor last night to ask me some questions. He doesn't seem to think a woman her size was capable of the murder."

"Yeah," Nick said, looking out the window to his right. It wasn't much of a view but his eyes had a glazed look that told me he wasn't really seeing anything anyway. "I'm sorry you got dragged into all of this, Holly."

"It's not your fault." I shrugged and took a casual sip of my coffee. "Is there anything I can do to help? What's going on with the case?"

"Not much right now. The police are still processing the evidence gathered at the scene and looking for the woman he was with. She's the best shot they have at finding a witness. They've already questioned the staff that were on duty that night and are combing through the security footage to see who else was on that floor around the time of the murder."

"How is Georgia taking all of this?"

"I don't know how she was when Chief Lincoln spoke with her, but she seems more or less the same as normal when I saw her. It was almost a little unnerving, to be honest. I mean, I understand they were preparing to divorce and weren't in love with each other anymore, but still ..." Nick stared off into space again, contemplating.

"It's so sad." I shook my head, just as confused by it as Nick appeared to be. "Could she think of anyone who would have wanted to hurt her husband?"

Nick shook his head. "There's always the possibility that whoever did this wasn't there for Paul. They could have been there for his date. Maybe they attacked her and Paul stepped into the middle of it to protect her. Of course, they'll have to process the DNA gathered at the scene to make sure all the blood was Paul's. If they find a second type ..." He didn't finish his sentence, but the meaning was obvious.

Nick dropped his gaze back to his desk and I noticed the spread of papers over the desk. He'd shoved his keyboard and computer mouse aside to make room for pictures and sticky notes. I saw the picture of Georgia and Paul that had been stored on Nick's phone the night we went to the hotel. I stared at the medallion around her neck and that same creeping suspicion washed over me. It was clear now that Paul wasn't a vampire. If he had been, the SPA would have swarmed the scene before the local cops could even get a peek. A dead vampire was not a sight fit for human eyes.

But, Paul *not* being a vampire only made me more curious as to how his wife had gotten ahold of a necklace bearing the symbol. Was there some chic boutique making a killing off Otherworldly symbols and markings? Or had it simply caught her eye at a flea market or vintage shop? There were a hundred ways she could have gained possession of it; if there was a simple explanation, I wanted to find it—and soon. I needed to quiet the nagging voice in the back of my mind that was whispering that something even more deadly than a mortal killer was loose in Beechwood Harbor.

CHAPTER 10

$\mathcal{I}$ left Nick's office feeling even more fired up than before. I had to get to the bottom of the necklace situation and there was only one person who could help me get some answers: Georgia Banks herself. But I had no idea how to convince her to talk to me. I couldn't take Nick with me and then go spouting off about vampires and ancient symbols. I had to go alone, but I had no way of knowing where Georgia and Paul Banks even lived.

I paused at the edge of the sidewalk and inspiration struck. Within five minutes, I had a large chocolate mocha in hand and was marching right back into Nick's office. He looked surprised to see me but I got a real smile out of him once he saw that I came bearing coffee. "Holly! You didn't have to do that."

"Well, I can't very well have Beechwood Harbor's best PI melting down. So a caffeine fix was in order." I handed over the coffee and when his fingers grazed the side of the cup I sloshed a little of the liquid. "Oh, bats!"

I'd used a sprinkle of magic to keep the liquid from

burning Nick's fingers but a stream dribbled down his hand. "Ahh!"

"Do you have paper towels?" I asked.

He shook his head and set the drink gingerly down on his desk. "I'll have to get some."

"I'm really sorry, Nick."

He headed for the door. "Don't worry about it. Be right back."

He slipped out into the hall to go down to the shared bathroom space and as soon as the door closed behind him, I sprang into action. I rummaged through the notes on his desk until I found Georgia's name and number. Underneath was a sticky note with an address. "Gotcha!" I whispered to myself. I scribbled the address down on a fresh note from the stack at the edge of his desk and stuffed it into my pocket. I waved my hand over the notes, sending a cleansing charm over them to dry the sticky mocha mess.

Nick came back in and offered me a handful of paper towels. I dried off the exterior of his cup and made a show of cleaning the desk before he took his seat. "Thanks, Holly."

"No problem. Enjoy." I started back to the door, eager to get going.

"Holly?"

I froze in place, my hand just reaching for the door knob. "Yes?"

"Have you seen my—" He stopped and lifted up a pen. "Never mind, here it is."

I heaved a sigh of relief, wiggled my fingers in his direction, and scurried from his office.

Once outside, I chucked my own empty coffee cup and hurried back to the manor. As I walked, I plugged the address into the GPS on my phone and started scanning the map for familiar landmarks nearby. I didn't have a car and didn't want to pay for a cab if it could be helped. It was easier—not to mention cheaper—to use the Larkspur neck-lace to *hop* to a familiar location nearby and walk the rest of the way. Luckily, the Banks' home was on a hillside over-looking the ocean. Adam and I had been to the little seaside restaurant that was just a few blocks away from the high end neighborhood, so I could visualize the restaurant and hop.

When I arrived at the manor, I didn't bother going inside. Instead, I headed for my greenhouse. Once safely inside, I looked up the name of the restaurant. JJ's Seafood Shanty. I remembered the outside of the restaurant—the white clap-board exterior and the blue door. I squeeze my eyes closed tightly, trying to think of a place to appear where no one would see me. It wasn't even noon yet, so unless they served breakfast, I wasn't in too much danger. But still … there was no point in taking the risk, especially not with Harvey breathing down my neck.

I locked onto the memory of the side patio and the fence that encircled it and whispered, "JJ's Seafood Shanty."

When I opened my eyes, I was crouched down behind the fence and smiled to myself. "Perfect."

From the restaurant, the Banks' home was a brisk walk. The way was a steep uphill incline and I arrived at their front door winded and slightly sweating. "Great, Holly. Perfect first impression."

I didn't have too long to agonize over the state of my appearance because before I could ring the doorbell, the front door opened and I found myself staring at Georgia Banks. I hopped back, teetering on the edge of the stairs that led to the porch. "Oh!"

"Who are you?" Her beautiful face pinched into a severe look. "Are you some kind of reporter? You leeches don't even have the common decency to give a grieving widow a chance to breathe!"

I held up my hands in surrender. "Mrs. Banks, please, I'm not a reporter. I swear."

She folded her arms and I noticed that she was dressed like she was going out for a date. She was wearing a clingy turquoise dress under an unbuttoned black overcoat. My eyes darted to her throat and I noted she was wearing the medallion. "If you're not a reporter, then who are you?"

Right, a cover story. That might have been helpful to make up before blitzing myself across town to confront the woman on a paper-thin hunch.

"Are you deaf?" Georgia snapped her fingers in front of my face.

Okay, enough was enough. I planted my fists on my hips. "No, I'm not. My name is Holly Boldt and I work with Nick Rivers." Georgia's expression softened slightly. "I'm here to ask a few questions about Mr. Banks."

"Nick already came by. I also gave a statement to the police chief. Landon or something."

"Lincoln," I corrected.

"Whatever." She flipped a hand at me. "They know everything already. I don't have anything new to share."

Georgia took a step backwards, ready to retreat into her house, and I held up a hand. "Does the name Molder mean anything to you?"

Her brown eyes widened a bit and her hand went to the shiny medallion at her throat before she could stop herself. "I don't know what you're talking about."

I arched an eyebrow. "Then why are you wearing the Thraxis?"

"How do you—I don't—" she stammered, her eyes sweeping back and forth as though expecting my backup to pop out of the bushes in her front yard. "Who are you?"

"Tell me where you got the necklace and I'll answer your questions."

She considered me for a moment and then took a hurried step back and waved a hand, ushering me inside her sprawling home. She closed and locked the door as soon as I crossed the threshold. The foyer was open to the second floor, with a large chandelier hanging overhead—real crystal from the look of it. Georgia's heels clicked on the marble flooring and I followed her through the house.

The only word that really came to mind was *lavish*. Pricey looking art adorned the walls and the marble floors beneath my feet were polished to a soft sheen. The kitchen and eating nook amounted to the same square footage as the entire first floor of the manor. Georgia appeared accustomed—suited, even—to the large home. Though it was hard to tell how old she was through her heavy makeup, I would have bet that she had barely five years on me. But just from the few minutes spent in her presence, it was obvious that our lives could not be more different.

"Tea?" Georgia offered, more as a social obligation.

I shook my head. "I won't take up much of your time, Mrs. Banks."

She gave me a nod and then licked her lips. "What I'm about to tell you can't leave this house. Do I have your word?"

"Of course."

Georgia considered me for a long moment and then continued, "I don't want to seem callous about my husband's death. But, as Nick has probably already mentioned, Paul and I were ready to part ways. It's why I hired Nick in the first place." She paused and dragged in a sigh. "When Paul and I met, we fell hard and fast for each other. We were engaged a year after we first met and married the year after that. We were young and stubborn. We thought we knew what we were doing…"

Her eyes drifted across the room and out the huge

windows above the kitchen sink. A large patio encircled what appeared to be an underground pool covered by a thick protective pad. "Things changed a few years ago. Paul was working more and more and taking extended trips out of town. Meanwhile, I was here, building a life for us both. But the life I was building wasn't what Paul wanted. We started falling apart, unraveling from the inside out. A few months ago, I was unpacking his suitcase when he got home from yet another trip and found lipstick marks on one of his shirts. That was when I went to Nick."

She dragged her gaze back to me. The spark was gone, leaving her eyes dull and listless. "Paul comes from money. I, on the other hand, do not. We have—*had*—an iron clad pre-nup. If we divorced, I'd be left with a lump sum that wouldn't be enough to even get me through a year."

"Unless he was cheating?"

Georgia nodded. "I wanted proof of what I already knew was going on. Shortly after hiring Nick, I came to terms with the fact that my marriage was over, and that's when I met Greyson."

A shiver snaked down my spine. "Greyson *Molder?*"

Georgia smiled slightly. "That's right."

Panic swirled through my stomach. This was so much worse than I'd imagined. Greyson Molder was a notorious vampire, nearly two hundred years old, and the heir to the Molder family.

"Greyson and I met and he opened my eyes to an entirely new world," Georgia said, her smile growing. She raised a hand to her necklace. "He gave me this necklace as a symbol of his promise."

"To?"

"Turn me," Georgia replied without blinking. "He sees that I'm meant for something better than spending my life being Paul's glorified maid."

"So, why not just leave Paul? The Molder family has more than enough money to keep you … comfortable. You didn't need Paul's money."

Georgia bristled at my question but she sighed impatiently and answered me, "It's a matter of principle. He can't just go around cheating on me with stewardesses and waitresses and expect to get away with it!"

"Got it." I pressed my lips together and resisted the urge to point out that her dalliance with Greyson Molder was likely putting her in a pot-kettle situation. "So you want to be a vampire? To be with Greyson?"

Georgia cocked her hip. "I've answered enough of your questions. Tell me who you are. How do you know about the Molders?"

I blew out a puff of air. This should be interesting … "Georgia, I don't know what Greyson has told you about the supernatural world he comes from, but I'm a witch. I used to live inside the Seattle haven but relocated here about a year ago."

"A witch." Georgia repeated.

"That's right. And let me tell you something—I've heard about the Molder House my entire life. They're an infamous vampire family. And not for doing charity work, Georgia."

She folded her arms.

"They are glamorous and decadent and I can understand why you would be attracted to that world, but Georgia, you have to know what you're getting yourself into—"

"I do! Greyson's already answered all my questions."

I resisted the urge to sigh. I was preaching to a deaf choir. Nothing I said would make a difference. She'd already made up her mind. "Listen, Nick doesn't know anything about the supernatural world. I'm sure Greyson has explained that humans can't know about this."

"I know," she said, sounding a little put-out at my sharp

reminder. "I'm not going to say anything. Who would believe me, even if I did?"

She had a point.

I pocketed my hands. "Good. So, it's safe to assume that Paul didn't know anything about this?"

Georgia shook her head and ran a finger over the etchings in the pendent. "I told him I found the necklace at a jewelry party one of my friends hosted."

"Right." I shifted my weight back onto my heels as my mind pedaled through the half a dozen scenarios in my mind. Had Georgia wanted Paul dead? It certainly didn't sound like it. But what if she'd said something in the heat of the moment and Greyson took it upon himself to *take care* of the problem? Then again, it was just as easy to teeter the other direction and assume that Paul's murder had nothing to do with the Molder family.

"I don't know who killed Paul, Ms. Boldt. But I can assure you it wasn't me. I have an airtight alibi and three friends who will back me up." She scoffed and tossed her long hair over her shoulder. "I'm sure Chief Landon is already running down security footage to prove I was at Le Blanc, an art gallery, thirty miles south of where Paul was found."

"I'm sure Chief *Lincoln* will double-check everything." I wasn't sure what unnerved me more, that the woman before me wanted to be turned into a vampire or the utterly breezy attitude she had towards the death of her husband.

"Is that everything then?" Georgia asked before making a show of consulting the silver—or, likely platinum—watch around her wrist. "I do have places to go."

"One last question," I replied, holding up a finger. "Where did you meet Greyson?"

"There's a club," she answered, suddenly looking a little shifty. "It's underground and kind of … gritty. Raven. A lot of vampires hang out there. Not that I knew that at the time. A friend took me."

"Just Raven?"

"Yes. Now, if you'll excuse me …"

I reached into the neckline of my sweater, tugged the Larkspur free, closed my eyes and whispered, "The greenhouse."

When my eyes fluttered open, I was surrounded by the familiar scent of all my plants and smiled to myself, wishing I could have seen the look on Georgia's face when I vanished right before her eyes.

CHAPTER 11

"*H*olly, how *do* you get yourself into these messes?" I muttered to myself as I bustled around the greenhouse. I'd never heard of an underground vampire club. According to Georgia, the elusive Raven was the best place to start my search for information, but I had no idea where to even start looking for it. Luckily, I knew someone who would. However, undead or not, beauty queens needed their sleep, and it wasn't likely that Lacey wasn't going to be in the mood to answer questions for at least a few more hours. Since I was still way behind on potion orders, I'd use that time to catch up. I needed to do some harvesting before heading over to Evangeline's spa to take over the back room for a potion brewfest.

Evangeline was thrilled to see me and quickly ushered me into the supply room after barking at everyone that I was not to be disturbed. I thanked her and dove into work as soon as she closed the door. The hours flew by as I whipped up potion after potion, restocking my supplies and working on custom orders for my ever-growing clientele. The town of Beechwood Harbor was growing rapidly—too rapidly according to most of the residents—but it seemed that more and more supernaturals were moving into the area, most of them coming over from the Seattle haven, which was only a few hours away. I wasn't sure whether it was the ocean views, the generally mild weather, or the charm of small town life bringing them in. Whatever it was that drew them into town, I was grateful. My business had been booming for the past few months and there were no signs of slowing down. Well at least not before Harvey's sudden appearance.

As I worked, I ran through all the facts of the case and replayed my strange visit with the late Mr. Banks' pretty wife. I hadn't been able to ask her all the questions rolling around in my mind, the most pressing of which was why she even wanted to become a vampire. She was young, rich, beautiful. She already had everything that most people coveted. So why was she still unhappy and searching for an escape? How had Greyson Molder sold her on the idea of giving up her mortal life? And why? Was it really love, or was there something else he wanted from her?

When I finished my work, I started to clean up the discarded fragments of plant material and other potion supplies. My stomach growled as I finished packing up my small trunk and I realized it was nearing five o'clock. Surely Lacey would be awake by now. And if she'd had a chance to have her first glass of fake blood, she might even be in the mood to talk. I tucked my potion supplies back into the cupboard Evangeline had assigned to me and double-checked that all my security wards were set.

I left the supply room and made my way down the hallway that led to the treatment rooms and pushed through the dark green curtain that separated the retail space from the spa rooms. Lacey was already there, sitting at Lucy's station, getting her nails painted a shocking shade of red. Figured. Evangeline was seated at the front desk talking on the phone, but she looked up as I stepped into the room and offered me a smile.

I waved at her on my way to join Lacey and Lucy.

"Hey, Holly," Lucy said. "You all done working?"

"Yeah. Hey, Lacey."

"Hello," she replied before continuing to blow on the nails of her finished hand. "You need to spend more time at the manor. Your cat is getting *clingy*."

I smiled. "Aww, are you two finally bonding?"

Lacey wrinkled her nose and shivered. She wasn't an animal person. Heck, most of the time she wasn't a *people* person.

"Adam should be coming back soon," I said. "That should get Bootsie off your case."

"More like my leg," she grumbled.

Lucy and I exchanged a look as we tried to control our giggles. "Trust me, Lacey; I would love to be able to do my work at home. I'm grateful to Evangeline for letting me work here, but the supply closet has nothing on the manor's kitchen. But with Harvey poking around, it just isn't possible."

"What does he even want?" Lucy asked.

I shrugged. "No idea. But the other night, Chief Lincoln came by to ask some questions about the murder—" I paused, wondering if they'd even heard about it. "You know about that, right?"

They both nodded and Lucy said, "It's all anyone can talk about. Some of the old-timers are saying the town's cursed."

I rolled my eyes. "Oh brother."

"Yeah."

Lucy finished Lacey's second hand and leaned back in her chair, rolling her wrists through the air to release the tension. "It'll blow over. Right?"

Lacey nodded. "Next week there will be some new

scandal to rave about. You know, someone cutting their grass before ten o'clock on a Saturday morning or a stray dog eating people's newspapers." She shifted her ice blue eyes to me and smiled. "After all, you said Adam was coming back soon, right?"

I snorted. "Don't make me stun you."

"Now, now, ladies," Lucy laughed.

I glanced around the room and spotted a woman in her mid-thirties consulting a bottle of shampoo. She looked lost in deep thought but I leaned in a little closer and lowered my voice just in case. "Anyway, when I finished talking to the chief, Harvey was there on the stairs and had apparently listened to the whole conversation. I told him off and he vanished into thin air."

"Really?" Lacey asked, sitting up a little straighter.

"Yeah. It was creepy."

"And you don't have any idea why he's here?" Lucy asked.

"Not a one," I replied grumpily.

Lucy frowned. "Well I hope he leaves soon. I'm going to need a double batch of Permasmile."

I raised my eyebrows. "Oh?"

"The monster-in-law is coming back to town in three weeks."

"What? Why? I thought she moved to Maine?"

"She did." Lucy shook her head, sending her shoulder-length black hair flying around her face. "But she was there for exactly two weeks before deciding the entire layout needed to be changed. And guess where she's staying while the work is being done."

I grimaced.

Lucy heaved a sigh. "Exactly."

I reached across the narrow table and patted her shoulder. Lucy's mother-in-law was constantly picking at her and even when she didn't say anything out loud, Lucy had the misfortune to overhear her every thought because she hadn't yet mastered her telepathy. She relied on my potion to keep her smiling and relaxed so that she wouldn't throttle the woman. "I'll have the potion ready for you tomorrow."

"Thanks, Holly. You're a lifesaver." She pushed up from her seat and added, "And I mean *hers*."

I laughed and gave her a nod. "I figured."

"Lacey, I'll go get set up for your facial," she said, heading for the green curtain.

"Thank you. I'll be there as soon as these are dry," Lacey replied, wiggling her freshly painted nails.

"Quite the day of beauty you're having here, huh?" I said, casually reaching for a magazine.

Lacey shrugged. "Why not?"

I flipped open the magazine and glanced over the top at the woman still agonizing over which shampoo to buy. Evangeline ended her phone call and swooped in to assist the woman. Once the two were lost in conversation, I turned to Lacey. "Have you heard of a vampire club called Raven?"

"Raven?" Lacey blinked, clearly surprised by my out-of-nowhere question. "Sure. It's not exactly the kind of place I hang out, but some of my friends like it."

I drew in a deep breath, wondering how much I should tell her. Normally when trying to puzzle out a case, I had Nick to bounce ideas and theories off of, but in this case, he had to be kept in the dark. "Okay, so long story short, the man who was murdered was married to a woman named Georgia Banks. She's been seeing Greyson Molder on the side for a few months now and he's agreed to turn her—"

"What?" Lacey snapped. "That's insane!"

I held up my hands. "Just the messenger."

"That's against the vampire code. Even a *Molder* would know that …," Lacey fumed. "This has to be reported to the Vampire Council."

"Vampire Council?"

Lacey sighed impatiently. "Yes. Some vampires prefer not to go through the Haven Council. Vampire matters are ... well, they're different than other supernaturals. Most vampires have been around longer than the haven system has even existed!"

I wasn't sure how I felt about another governing system running under the radar of the one put into place for *all* supernaturals, but I wasn't going to argue about it with Lacey. At least not before I had all the information. Still, it was disconcerting that I'd never even heard of the Vampire Council and had spent the majority of my life living among supernaturals.

I pushed my hair back and puffed out a breath. "Okay, well, he hasn't done the turning yet, but what I need is information. See, Nick is tangled up in this case. Georgia was his client and he feels responsible to get to the bottom of it. Obviously I can't tell him to stay out of the way, but I can't just sit back either. He has no idea what he's up against! If a Molder killed Paul Banks ..."

Lacey finished my thought, "They would have no problem killing anyone who got in the middle of it."

A shiver snaked up my spine as I nodded in agreement. "I can't let that happen."

She turned to me. "I'll see what I can find out."

"Thank you, Lacey. I really appreciate it."

She swept up from her seat. "Just keep that cat away from me."

I rolled my eyes as she stalked to the back room to continue her beautification. Evangeline was still busy with her customer, so I waved to her and mouthed my goodbye as I left the spa. I burrowed into my coat and hurried back up the hill to the manor. Boots would be howling for dinner by now and no one would be there to feed him. My own rumbling stomach agreed that dinner was a good idea. I also needed to call Adam and see if he was coming back tonight or in the morning.

When I walked in, the manor was quiet for half a heartbeat, then a raging tabby shattered the peace with an earsplitting howl before I even got the front door closed. A pair of glowing amber eyes appeared in the shadows at the end of the hallway and I knew I was in deep trouble. "Boots, I'm sorry!" I said, kneeling down on the welcome mat. I extended a hand, trying to coax him near, but he continued to glare at me. "Okay, okay, message received. Food now, apologies later. Got it."

I pushed up from the floor, kicked out of my boots, and shrugged out of my coat. Boots didn't race ahead, as per his custom, but instead followed me from a few feet's distance as though supervising me to make sure I didn't deviate from the course. I hurried to get him a bowl of food, spoiling him with the entire contents of the can, instead of just a half. Only after he finished stuffing his fluffy face did he come over and let me pet him.

"Holly?"

The sound of Posy's voice startled me and, in my squatted position, I nearly lost my balance. I steadied myself with a hand on the side of the cupboards and craned around to see her silvery silhouette solidify near the stove. "Hi, Posy. How are you?"

"I'm fine, dear. I came to tell you there's someone outside. That PI friend of yours."

"Nick's here?" I pushed up from the floor after giving Boots a final pat on the head.

The doorbell rang.

"He doesn't look too happy," Posy added before she shimmered and floated back through the kitchen door.

"Great," I said with a sigh. I headed out of the kitchen and let the door flap closed behind me. Boots would likely go and curl up in his cat bed and spend the next hour grooming himself. "Posy, do you know where Harvey is?"

"Mr. Colepepper? No, dear. I haven't seen him today, although the door to his room is closed. I suppose he could still be in there. I expect he's off doing important SPA work."

"I suppose …" I gave a withering glance at the stairs and hoped he wouldn't pop into view while Nick was here. "Thanks, Posy."

Posy vanished up through the ceiling and I opened the front door. She hadn't been exaggerating. Nick was wearing a scowl so deep I feared he was etching permanent wrinkles into his face. "Nick?"

"What were you thinking, Holly? What gave you the right?" he fumed, stepping into the manor without an invitation.

I closed the door and whirled around to face him. "Slow down, Nick. What are you talking about?"

He crossed his arms. "Why did you go interrogate Georgia?"

I reared back as though he'd landed a physical slap. "What?" I spat.

So much for not dragging Nick into it.

Nick glared at me. "She called me this evening and told me that I needed to call off my—well—I won't use her exact language, but she told me all about your little visit."

My heart slammed against my chest. "*All* about?" I repeated. Harvey was going to kill me. A human finding out about the supernaturals in Beechwood Harbor would be unforgivable. Un-sweep-under-the-rug-able.

"She said you drilled her for information about Paul and she had to demand that you leave."

I scoffed and rolled my eyes up at the ceiling even as a surge of relief spread over me. At least she'd kept her word about not bringing up the whole witch thing. "That's ridiculous, Nick."

"So she's just making up the whole thing?" he asked, leveling me with another harsh glare.

"No." I paused and dragged a hand through my hair. "No, she's not making it up. I did go see her. I just wanted to ask her a few questions about Paul and see if she had thought of anything that might help us."

Nick's jaw flexed. "Why? You don't think I'm doing everything I can to get to the bottom of this? You thought I needed your help?"

"I didn't mean anything by it, Nick. I thought I could help. That's all. I promise."

He threw his hands up in the air.

"Nick, please," I stammered, closing the gap between us. "I've helped you before and thought I might be able to lend another pair of eyes."

Nick took a step back, out of reach. "Just stay out of this, Holly."

His anger surprised me. Nick and I had successfully solved two murders over the past year and regularly joked about me going to work for him as a junior PI. Beyond that, we were friends.

"I'm sorry, Nick."

He stormed back to the front door. "You might have meant well, Holly. But Georgia just fired me and is refusing to pay me because she thinks I broke her confidence. Your whim, or instinct to help, or whatever it was, just cost me a big job and I have no doubt that Georgia will share her experience with her friends. A woman like that has pull, especially in a town this small. This could cost me my entire business, Holly."

I was speechless. My mouth opened and closed but nothing came out. Nick didn't wait for me to rally. He wrenched the door open and stalked out into the night. Only once he was gone did a few tears slip past my lashes. I had no idea how I would fix it, but I knew I had to.

I dragged myself back to the kitchen to finish making myself something to eat, although my stomach was churning and I was no longer hungry. As I pushed the door open, I heard something rustling around. My jaw hit the floor when I stepped inside and found Harvey elbow deep in my messenger bag, his stubby fingers wrapped around two potion vials that I'd filled while working at Evangeline's.

No, no no.

Harvey's eyes were dark as they flicked up to me. "Well, well, well." A cruel smile twisted his features. "What do we have here, Holly Boldt? Back to your old tricks, I see."

CHAPTER 12

"*H*arvey," I exclaimed, surging into the kitchen. I raised my hand, ready to summon the bag and vials away from him, but I wasn't fast enough. He snapped his fingers and my wrists slapped together in front of me. I tugged and twisted but there was nothing I could do. The magic encircled my wrists as tight as if I were physically cuffed. I couldn't break free. "Harvey, no! Please, don't do this. I can explain!"

He chuckled. "Oh, I'll just bet. Holly, in all the years we've known each other, you've always had a good excuse. Last time you were in cuffs, I went out of my way to give you a second chance, and now I can see that all of your promises were meaningless. I've already tested these potions. They're marked with your signature. There's no way you can deny you were the master who produced them."

I bit down into my lip to keep myself from crying. "Harvey, please, it's harmless—"

"Enough!" he snapped. "I'm taking you back to the Seattle haven and I'm leaving you there. I'm in the middle of an investigation here and don't have time to debate this with you. Now, let's go."

Boots sprang into action, leaping for Harvey, but he blocked him with a shield. Boots hissed and stood between Harvey and me. "Bootsie, it's okay," I said, no longer able to keep the tears back. They coursed down my cheeks as I looked down at Boots. He swiveled his amber eyes up to me and blinked slowly. He understood. The bond between a witch and her familiar was a powerful thing. He would fight to the death for me, if needed, but he understood when I was beyond his help. "I'll be all right. You stay here. Adam will take care of you." At the thought of Adam, my tears quickened. I closed my eyes and drew in a deep breath. I rarely cried, and breaking down in front of Harvey was the last thing I wanted to do. I had to get it together and be strong. For myself. For Boots.

But it was impossible. The thought of being dragged out of the manor and never coming back was too much for me to take. I couldn't leave. Adam, Posy, Lacey, Evangeline, and Cassie were all my family now. And Nick. My heart twisted painfully at the thought of Nick. I'd wrecked the case and potentially damaged his business. What would happen to him? The only small consolation was that if Georgia really fired him, he'd stay out of the investigation and be out of the path of danger.

"Let's go, Boldt." Harvey demanded. "We'll use the SPA portal to get back to the city. I can get you booked in time to make it back before bed."

"How nice for you," I replied, glaring down at him.

He shrugged, unruffled by my sharp tone.

Boots rubbed against my legs and I whispered, "Be good, Bootsie."

As Harvey walked ahead, I felt a tug at my wrists. The invisible bonds around my wrists would pinch until I took a step if Harvey got too far ahead of me. It was like a magically enforced leash. I followed him out of the kitchen and through the living room. I looked around, wishing Posy would appear so that I could tell her what was happening. I still had no idea when Adam was coming back, but she could explain to the others and make sure Boots was looked after. But there was no sign of her. She was likely in the attic, listening to her favorite record over and over again.

Harvey opened the door and a blast of cold air swelled inside the entry way. I was about to demand that he release the spell long enough for me to put a coat on, but the words died on my lips as I realized voices were filtering up the walk. Adam!

Wait.

Two other voices. One deep and masculine. The other high and fast.

My stomach plummeted. "No," I whispered. "No, it can't be …"

Adam appeared, a huge smile on his face, completely overlooking the goblin lurking by the door. "There she is! Gorgeous, look who decided to come a few days early." He turned and I squeezed my eyes closed, wishing myself away. If I could have gotten ahold of the Larkspur, I would have vanished to some far away island. Anywhere would be better than the humiliation of what was happening right in front of me. "Holly, this is—"

I forced my eyes open and saw Adam standing next to a man who looked exactly like him, except he was a few inches shorter and a few pounds heavier, with salt and pepper hair and far better taste in clothing. In front of him was a woman in a posh red coat, black dress, and cherry-red heels that perfectly matched her coat. She had shiny, raven hair, deep green eyes, and rosy cheeks.

"—my dad, Mort, and my mother, Bella."

"What a lovely little introduction," Harvey's gravelly voice interjected. Adam and his parents all swiveled to face Harvey, obviously just seeing him for the first time, as he came out from behind the door. "Unfortunately, Holly is a little too busy for a family reunion right now."

Adam looked at me, concern etched in his face. His eyes dropped to my wrists and went wide as he realized they were pinned together. "What's going on, Holly?"

"Harvey found some vials—"

Adam's shoulders tensed and he rounded on Harvey. "You little—"

"Adam! Don't!" I said.

Mort stepped forward. "I'm sorry, but who are you?"

Harvey snapped his fingers and like a slight-of-hand trick, a silver card appeared. He handed it to Adam's father. "Harvey Colepepper. SPA. And as I said, Ms. Boldt and I have somewhere to be. If you want to see her, you can all come visit her at the Seattle Haven Prison once I get her booked for illegal potion work. Goodnight."

Adam raced to me and wrapped his arms around me. I melted into him and started to cry again. "Take care of Boots," I whispered. "He's terrified."

"Of course." Adam nodded. "I'll get you out, Holly. Don't say anything to anyone."

"Get Evangeline to call her friend. Teddy something or other."

"I will."

"Mr. St. James," Harvey said.

Adam squeezed me tight and kissed me before releasing me. I found myself staring at his open-mouthed parents and felt my cheeks warm. Great first impression, Holly.

Harvey moved quickly considering that his legs were less than half the length of my own. He barreled down the sidewalk and I dragged behind, only taking steps when the tension around my wrists became unbearable or he barked out an order. He stopped at the corner and I craned around to take one last long look at the manor.

Then, with a snap of his fingers, it was gone.

~

"HARVEY, you have to listen to me."

We were still in Beechwood Harbor, but with a click on his fingers, we'd landed on the other side of town. Harvey wasted no time barreling toward his destination, not stopping to address my pleas or answer any of my questions. We walked for a few minutes in cold silence through a neighborhood, staying in the shadows between street lights. Harvey walked up to an older home, bypassing the front door entirely, and went to a cellar door on the side.

"Where are we? Whose house is this?"

Harvey sighed. "Enough questions, Holly. This is happening. Whether you like it or not, or think it's fair." He stopped to square off against me and folded his arms. "Back in Seattle, I stuck my neck out for you against my better judgment. You swore to me that you were done playing potions master and I believed you. I *wanted* to believe you. For whatever reason, I have a soft spot for you."

I blinked rapidly. Soft spot? I shuddered to think how this night would play out if he didn't claim some affection for me.

"I can't let this slide, Holly. There are laws put in place by the council. And those laws are meant to help and protect. Why couldn't you just petition the council for your potions master license and go through the process like every other potions master? Why do you insist on making things so difficult for yourself and everyone else?"

I frowned down at him. "Are you actually being serious right now?"

He didn't reply.

"Harvey, you know that there is no way in this world or the Other that the council would grant me my potions master license. Not with my connection to Gabriel. Not to mention my last name. When was the last time a Boldt woman ever held a position of power?"

"Your aunt has done well for herself," he pointed out.

"That's because she married that awful SPA councilman. If not for that, she'd be back in the house she had when I was growing up, doing side jobs to make ends meet, and doing her best to scrape together enough money to take care of me."

Harvey sighed and dropped his arms. The motion reminded me of a deflating balloon. Maybe I was finally getting through to him. Just maybe.

"Harvey, you know I'm not hurting people. My potions *help* people. Supernaturals. Potions that help grandfathers ignore their back pain to play on the floor with their grandchildren, potions to help students remember the things they read in their textbooks so they can do well in school, even a potion to help keep a telepath from killing her nasty mother-in-law! Surely those things all earn me some small level of grace here."

My heart pounded so loud I could hear it in my ears as a long moment spanned between us. But finally, Harvey reached for the cellar door. "It's too late, Holly. I have to do my job. This is a portal that will take us to the SPA station inside the Seattle haven. I'll make sure to put in a good word for you so that maybe you won't spend the rest of your life in a windowless cell. But that's all I can do. Then I'm done. I have my own career to worry about."

He tugged the handle and opened the door. Instead of a dank cellar, a flood of purple shone from the other side. I'd never used this type of portal before—they were usually reserved for government officials—but I imagined it wasn't much different than the gateway between the human version of Seattle and the paranormal community that lay just under the surface.

"Wait! Harvey, you're here about the Molders aren't you?" The question flew from my mouth before I could reconsider it. It was a desperate move. "You know they're turning humans. That's why you're in Beechwood Harbor!"

Harvey's beady eyes went so wide I thought they would pop out of his head, and my heart flipped. I was right. "How do you know about that?"

I extended my cuffed hands. "Let me out of these and I'll tell you all about it."

"Holly, I—"

"Harvey, who does the council want more? Me or the vampires responsible for turning humans? Which is more dangerous? I can help you solve your case. In exchange for my information, you let me go. Don't turn me in."

To my surprise, Harvey let the door handle slip from his hand and I flinched as it slammed back into place. "And your potion business?"

I chewed my lower lip. I couldn't lie to him again. He'd be watching me even closer if he let me return to the manor. I swallowed hard and ignored the stinging in my eyes. "If you let me fill the orders I have open, then I'll tell my customers that I'm going out of business."

Harvey studied me, as though he had the power of being a human—err, goblin—lie detector test. After a moment, he gave a solemn nod. "You have a deal, Holly. But if you cross me again, I'll make sure you spend the rest of your days inside a cell."

I swallowed. "I understand."

Harvey clicked his fingers and my cuffs fell away. I rubbed my wrists as he reopened the portal. "Come on, we'll discuss this at my office in the haven. There will be fewer distractions."

Thinking of Adam and his parents back at the manor made my stomach flop. I was thankful I wasn't going to jail. At least, not tonight. But the thought of going back and facing them again was more than I could bear. Harvey didn't give me long to wallow in self-pity, though. He guided me through the portal and we arrived in a long hallway inside a building I'd never seen before. Harvey didn't explain anything along the way, but it didn't take me long to piece together that we were inside the Seattle Haven SPA head-quarters.

He led the way to his office; a large, sprawling room that boasted a fantastic view of the supernatural city below. The space had an old-world charm that I never would have asso-ciated with the seemingly cold SPA agent. It was decorated with dark woods, rich tapestries, and books that looked older than both of us combined, though to be fair, I didn't have a clue whether Harvey was 50 or 500. He called his assistant to get us tea and once we'd been served and his assistant was gone, he waved a hand at the door, shutting and locking it.

Once we were alone, he leaned forward and braced his arms on his desk. He must have been seated on a pillow because he appeared far taller than usual and almost *stately* behind his large antique desk. "All right, tell me everything you know from the beginning," he said before slipping on a pair or horn rimmed glasses.

I took a long sip from the chamomile tea and then launched into the whole sordid story; everything from the stakeout with Nick to the confrontation with Georgia. I relayed what Lacey had told me about the Raven and the Vampire Council. None of it seemed to shock or startle Harvey. He listened carefully, only interjecting to ask a couple of follow-up questions along the way. When I finished, he leaned back in his chair and laced his fingers together in front of him. "We've known about the Vampire Council for some time. Regarding your friend, may I assume it was Lacey Vaughn?"

I frowned. "I said no names."

He shrugged as though it didn't concern him. "In any case, not *all* vampires prefer the ruling of the Vampire Council. However, there are enough of them that it does create problems from time to time. What interests me more is the medallion you saw on this woman, Georgia Banks. Do you think you could describe it to a crafter?"

My brow furrowed but I nodded. "Sure."

"Good. I'll set that up right away."

"Then I can go back home? My friends will be worried about me."

Harvey gave me an impatient look. "You'll go back when I'm good and ready to take you back."

I sighed. "Great."

Harvey leapt down from his place behind the desk and left the office. Once he was gone, I let out a frustrated growl. I didn't have my phone on me and I didn't have anyone's phone numbers memorized, so I couldn't use Harvey's phone. Knowing him, he had it charmed to lash out and attack anyone else who attempted to use it anyway, so maybe it was for the best.

I didn't have to wait for long. Harvey came back a few minutes later with a man in royal blue robes. He looked like he was a thousand years old and spoke in a voice so soft I had to practically embrace him to hear what he was saying. "Holly, this is Mr. Willows. He's the Seattle haven's best crafter. I need you to describe the medallion in detail and he will conjure a reproduction."

Crafters were a specific class of wizards who had the

ability to spin their magic into any physical item. Large parts of the havens were in existence because of crafters' work. "All right. But Harvey, what's so special about the medallion? Why does it matter?"

Harvey narrowed his eyes at me. "That's none of your concern, Holly. You just help Mr. Willows and then I'll take you home."

It rankled that he wouldn't tell me anything even after I'd been so candid with him. Harvey helped Mr. Willows into a chair and I took the one opposite him. After we began, Harvey slipped from the room. I described the necklace to Mr. Willow, who used his fingers to spin thin air into a gleaming replica of the necklace I'd last seen around Georgia Banks' neck. He handed it to me and I turned it over, inspecting it. "It's perfect."

As we were finishing, Harvey returned and snatched the medallion from me. He gave it a once over, then turned to the ancient crafter. "All right. Thank you, Mr. Willows." He pocketed the necklace and then turned back toward me. "Holly, let's go."

"You don't have to ask me twice."

rue to his word, Harvey took me back through the portal. We arrived back at the manor at half past midnight and he walked beside me up to the front door. He stopped short of opening it and turned to me. "Holly?"

"Yes?"

"Everything we discussed tonight needs to be kept completely confidential," he started. His expression and tone were so grave that I was taken aback. "This investigation is bigger than I can even begin to explain. Any leaks of information could bring the whole thing crashing down."

"I understand."

He eyed me skeptically. "Good, because months—years—of hard work are at stake."

I turned the handle and Harvey took a few steps backward. "Aren't you coming inside?" I asked.

He shook his head. "No. I won't be staying here anymore. I need to be back at headquarters, working from the inside to see what I can track down. I'll have my assistant drop by tomorrow to collect my belongings."

"Oh. Okay." I shifted, unsure what else to say.

"Finish your orders and notify your customers that they will need to find alternate arrangements for their potion needs."

I gave a miserable nod. "I will."

"Good." He nodded and pocketed his hands, burrowing them deep inside his coat. "You'll keep an eye out for any other oddities?"

"You'll be my first call."

"See to it that I am." He turned away and I pushed open the front door. Harvey stopped short and spun back around. My heart sank. He'd changed his mind. He was going to cuff me and drag me off again. Instead, he said, "Holly, when this is all done, I think you should go to the Haven Council and seek your potions master license."

"Harvey, I told you—"

"I'll testify on your behalf."

For the second time that night, I was rendered completely speechless.

"I know some of the council members personally, and can put in a good word for you. If what you said is true, about the good you're doing here, I don't think they will have a problem issuing a license."

"Wow. Uh ... thank ... thank you, Harvey. I don't know what to say," I stammered.

He held up a hand. "Don't thank me yet. This isn't over. Not by a long shot."

"Right."

He turned and continued down the walk and seconds later, a snap cracked through the night and he was gone.

I hesitated on the porch, one hand on the door knob, as I stared out into the night. My breath made little plumes in the cold air and I was bone tired, but I couldn't slow my racing thoughts. What was Harvey going to do back at the SPA office that he couldn't do here in Beechwood Harbor? What was going on with the Molder family? Why did he want a replica of Georgia's necklace? And, possibly most pressing, would I really have a shot at getting my potions license with his recommendation?

An icy wind kicked up and drove me inside. Suddenly all thoughts of the case and the strange conversation at Harvey's office fell away as I recalled that Adam's parents had seen me dragged out of the manor in SPA cuffs just a few hours earlier. Nick was furious with me and possibly in danger of losing his business, and my poor familiar was probably worried sick about me.

Posy was the first one to find me. "Holly? Holly! You're back for good?"

I wished she wasn't a ghost so I could give her a bear hug. "You can't get rid of me that easily," I quipped, smiling at her.

She laughed. "That's the best news I've heard in a hundred years, dear."

"Thanks, Posy."

Footsteps sounded and we were joined by Evangeline, Lacey, Adam, and Boots. A chorus of excitement was followed by a barrage of questions. I scooped Boots into my arms and buried my face in his fur before I started answering their questions.

"Where did you go?" Evangeline asked.

Adam waited until I set Boots back on the floor to wrap me in his arms. "Are you all right? If anyone laid a finger on you ..."

"Where's that pint-sized goblin?" Lacey demanded, her fangs bared.

I laughed softly. "Harvey took me to the Seattle haven. We made a little deal."

"A deal?" Adam repeated, his brows knit together.

I nodded. "I'm helping him with his case and in exchange, he let me go."

Evangeline cocked her head. "Just like that?"

"Well, not exactly." I dropped a look to my boots. "I have to shut down my potions business. For good this time, unless I can manage to get my license."

"Oh, Holly," she said. "I'm so sorry."

"Thank you. I guess in comparison to jail time, it's a bargain, but it hurts."

Adam squeezed me tighter. "We'll figure something out, gorgeous. I'm just glad you're back and you're safe."

"We all are," Posy added.

"Thanks you guys."

Evangeline embraced me when Adam let me go. "I've already called Teddy. He'll be here as soon as he can to help us sort all this out."

"I appreciate that, Evangeline, but I don't think there's much he can do at this point. But, Harvey did say that when this is all over, he'll help me petition the council to give me my license. So maybe Teddy can help with that?"

"Of course!" she said brightly, as though it were already a done deal.

"I'm glad you're back," Lacey said. "Things wouldn't be the same without you around here."

I sniffled, trying to hold in the swell of emotions that had been building in my chest for hours, but the dam broke and I burst into ugly tears.

~

"So on a scale from one to ten, how awkward is breakfast with your parents going to be tomorrow?" I asked Adam once we were alone again. Posy had gone up to the attic and Lacey and Evangeline had each retired to their own rooms. Adam and I went to the kitchen, Boots in hot pursuit, and I gave him a can of tuna to soothe him.

Adam chuckled from his place at the stove as he made two cups of hot apple cider. He brought them over to the table, steam pouring off them, and settled into the chair kitty-corner to mine at the end of the table. "I'd give it a solid eight and a half."

I groaned and dropped my head to the table. "Great."

Adam ran a hand over my shoulders. "It'll be fine. We'll just tell them …," he paused and I peeked up at him. His face was twisted into an expression that would have had me laughing out loud under any other circumstances. "We'll think of something."

I pushed up and propped my chin in my hands. "Adam, your parents just saw me hauled out of here in cuffs, led by an angry SPA goblin on a power trip. I'm not sure that's something we can just explain away. And even if we could, it's not going to scrub the visual from their minds."

"I know." He stirred the contents of his mug and frowned.

"I'm really sorry," I said, barely above a whisper. "This is all my fault. I should have followed the rules when I got into town. I never should have started my business back up again. It was always a gamble. At the beginning, it would have only affected me if I got busted. But now … well that's different, isn't it? Now my choices affect way more than just myself. I shouldn't have put any of you in that position."

Adam took my hand and offered me a smile. "Don't apologize, gorgeous. Your stubbornness is wildly attractive. At least when it's not directed at me." I laughed and he leaned forward to steal a kiss. "We'll figure something out and my parents will just have to deal. It's not like you murdered someone."

"Speaking of …"

Adam's eyebrows shot up.

I waved my hand. "Harvey's still alive and kicking, I promise. What I was going to say, is that this whole thing traces back to that case I was telling you about on the phone the other night."

"The Molder thing?"

I nodded and stirred my own cider. "Yeah. I can't really get into all the details. Harvey told me it's pretty top secret stuff and honestly, I'm not even really sure what the SPA is trying to accomplish, but it's a big deal and the only reason he let me go was because I agreed to help him and give him all the information I have."

"Bats, Holly."

"I know. Not ideal, but it was a last ditch effort that paid off."

He considered his still-steaming mug for a long moment. I could almost see the gears in his mind turning, but had no idea what they were churning over. "I just want you to be safe, Holly. All these murder cases with Nick—"

"Adam," I groaned.

"No, I'm serious, Holly. This isn't some over-zealous lady with a bottle of peppermint syrup in a back alley. This is really scary stuff! The Molders are ancient and they haven't survived this long by handing out lollipops and teddy bears."

"Don't you think I know that?"

He reached for my other hand and held on tightly. His dark eyes locked with mine. "Holly, promise me you'll leave this alone. You'll let the SPA take care of this mess and you won't go off half-cocked."

"Half-cocked? It's like you don't know me at all," I teased, desperate to break the thick mood between us.

Adam didn't so much as grin.

"Okay, okay. I promise. I'll leave it alone. I won't dig. I will go about my business."

"Thank you."

I shrugged. "It's for the best. Now that my business has been shut down, I need to find a second job."

A mischievous smile twitched at Adam's lips. "Too bad I don't have the budget to hire an assistant," he said, wiggling his thick brows at me.

I rolled my eyes to the ceiling but couldn't help but giggle at his suggestion.

~

WITH ONE CRISIS AVERTED, I set out early the next morning to solve the other. I stopped at Siren's Song to load up on goodies, even though I knew there was no way I would be able to worm my way back into Nick's good graces even with white chocolate chip cookies and a huge mocha with extra sprinkles. But, knowing Nick, it would be a good ice breaker to keep him from slamming the door of his office in my face.

And I was right. He was in his office, hunched over his desk, when I pushed open the door. He jumped when I stepped into the room, so lost in his own thoughts that he hadn't heard me tapping on the door seconds before I let myself in.

"Holly, what are you doing here?" He glanced up at the clock on the wall. It was barely seven o'clock and he didn't look like his mood had improved since the last time I'd seen him.

I cocked my hip. "The better question is what are *you* doing here? Do you ever sleep?"

Nick rubbed his eyes and then scrubbed his hands down his face. He looked haggard. A five o'clock shadow coated his cheeks and jawline and his hair was mussed from raking his hands through it. He was wearing a fresh shirt and different tie than the day before, but I still imagined he hadn't gone home for more than just a nap and a quick shower since the day before. He was always like this when there was a murder case on the line. I'd witnessed it twice before. He wasn't a cop, but he would work just as hard to get to the bottom of what had happened. It was the combination of the PI and reporter in him. It wouldn't quit.

"I come bearing gifts," I said, not waiting for him to answer the first question. I set the coffee and bag of cookies on the desk in front of him. "Although, considering you probably haven't eaten anything of substance since yesterday, I probably shouldn't drop this sugar bomb on you."

Nick swiped up the coffee cup before I could take it away. "Holly, sit down."

I did as he asked and slowly turned my own coffee cup, rolling it between my palms as I waited for him to speak.

"I'm sorry for yesterday," he said. "I shouldn't have come to your house and shouted at you like that."

"Nick, you don't—"

He stopped me with a hand. "No, let me finish, please."

"All right."

He dragged a hand through his hair. "We've known each other long enough now that I know you were trying to help. I also know you're a little … impulsive." I frowned at his assessment and a tiny hint of a smile crossed his lips before he hurried to add, "But I also know that your instincts are solid and usually right on."

I leaned back in my chair. "I should have told you I was going to visit Georgia. She's your client."

"*Was*," Nick corrected.

"Right." I shifted in my seat. "I crossed a line and I'm sorry, Nick. Is there anything I can do to help? I can go apologize to her too, if you think that would help."

Nick smiled and took a long drink of his mocha. "I think it's a little past that. But, I'm going to the hotel today to see about getting some more leads. You wanna tag along?"

"You really want me to?"

He shrugged. "Why not? Like I said, your instincts are usually dead on and I find it helps to bat around ideas."

"What are you looking for at the hotel? If you're not working for Georgia anymore, why bother?"

"Chief Lincoln has a theory he wants me to check out. As you know, he's low on manpower and asked me to follow up on his suspicions to see if anything turns up. Also, Georgia has offered up a substantial reward for information leading to the arrest of her late husband's killer." Nick smiled. "I guess she figured it was the right move to make. Although, if you ask me, it's more to garner attention to herself. Anyway, I figure if I'm not getting my stipend from her directly, then the reward money would be the next best thing."

"How much are we talking?"

"A cool 100K."

My mouth dropped open and Nick laughed. "Exactly. So, what do you say? You help me out, I'll give you a 30% cut. You working today?"

I popped up from my chair. "I am now! Let's go!"

Nick laughed and stood from his desk. He grabbed his coat from the rack and shrugged into it. "I thought that might sway you."

Technically I should probably go back to the manor and try to wow Adam's parents and make them forget about that whole dragged-out-in-handcuffs thing. But that idea was daunting and going with Nick sounded like a lot more fun. I'd promised Adam I would stay out of the SPA investigation, and definitely far away from any Molder family members, but asking some questions of a few hotel staffers couldn't be dangerous. Besides, if Nick and I cracked the case, my split of the reward money would go a long way toward softening the financial blow from shutting down my potions business.

Adam would understand.

CHAPTER 14

We arrived at the hotel caffeinated and slightly sugar high thanks to the tag-team effort on the bag of cookies during the drive over. Nick led the way to the front desk where a young woman dressed in black was studying a computer screen with a glazed look. Nick cleared his throat and placed his palms on the smooth stone countertop. "Excuse me."

The woman looked up, vaguely frowning. Clearly not a morning person. *Maybe I should introduce her to Lacey.* "Yes?"

Nick bristled at her impatient tone. "My name is Nick Rivers. I'm a PI working with the Beechwood Harbor PD on the murder investigation. I have some questions I'd like to ask the staffers who were on duty that night. Are any of them here today, by chance?"

She consulted her computer screen and the sound of her clicking mouse was the only thing that broke the silence. *I was starting to think that she was playing solitaire and ignoring our presence entirely* when she looked back up at

Nick. "You can talk to Ginger and Francine. They were working that night and are just finishing their shift now."

Nick nodded, making a mental note of the names. "And where might I find them?"

"Laundry room on the second floor."

"Thank you for your help," Nick said politely. When we were a few paces away, he looked at me archly. "Well. She was delightful."

I laughed under my breath and followed him onto the elevator. Once the door closed, I asked, "Did the police talk to these two women before?"

Nick shrugged. "I don't know. I would imagine so, but it never hurts to go back a few days after the event and get a second round of questions answered. A lot of times people don't think they saw anything, only to remember something later. Even something small, an odd detail or tiny fragment of information, can break a case wide open."

"I hope so." I wasn't convinced that the Molders weren't somehow linked to the case, but if it turned out they weren't responsible for the murder, it would make life easier, and infinitely safer, for everyone.

Nick motioned me off the elevator first and we wandered around the second floor of the hotel in search of the laundry room. Two women came rushing out of a door, coats in hand, and nearly crashing into us. Behind them were see washers, dryers, and a folding table. Apparently we'd found the girls from the laundry room or, more accurately, they'd found us.

"Are you lost?" the taller of the two women asked politely. She had long blonde hair that was pulled back in a low pony-tail, and wore understated make-up. Her name tag identified her as Ginger.

"No, ma'am. We're actually here to talk to you both," Nick replied.

The shorter woman had a dirty blonde pixie cut. She cocked a hip and looked at him suspiciously. "You a cop?"

I shifted a glance over to Nick. "Why is that always the first question?"

He ignored me and answered the girl. "I'm a private investigator. My name is Nick. I work with Chief Lincoln and his department on cases from time to time and am here to ask a few questions about the night of the unfortunate attack here in the hotel. The woman at the front desk said that both of you were working that night. I assume you're Francine?"

The shorter woman nodded and looked up at Ginger. Ginger took the lead and waved a hand at the door. "Let's get out of here. I've had enough of the humidity for one day. We're both off the clock now but we can answer your questions."

The clear message—make it quick.

Ginger led us to a small alcove that held a couple of wing-back chairs, a coffee table with magazines splayed across it, and some fake plants. "What do you want to know?" she asked. "We both spoke to the police when they were here … cleaning things up." She looked a little green just mentioning it.

Nick cleared his throat. Neither of us had seen the crime scene, but from what everyone was saying, I was grateful to have missed it. "Had you ever seen the victim here before that night?"

Ginger shook her head. "No, but our work keeps us in the laundry room for most of the night. I'm sure you can imagine the work load in a place like this. We have over a hundred rooms and stay pretty busy, especially this time of year with people coming in for the holidays."

"At least we *were* busy," added Francine.

Ginger nodded. "We've had a lot of cancellations since this happened."

An unfortunate side effect. I wondered if that explained the clerk's frosty reception at the desk. No paying guests, and probably a horde of looky-loos trying to find out what happened.

"Well the sooner we can get this cleared up, the sooner it will go back to normal." Nick retrieved a printed picture from inside his coat. It was the clearest one he had from the night we'd been out in the parking lot. Paul was tangled up with his mystery date. It was a haunting image in hindsight. "As you might have heard, the victim was here with a guest that night. She's missing. Do either of you recognize her?"

The two women studied the picture for a moment and then exchanged another dark look.

"What?" I interjected, a coil of anxiety wrapping around my stomach. "You know who she is?"

Francine sighed. "That's Naomi Givens. She's a—"

"Hooker," Ginger finished.

Nick flinched. "You're sure?"

"Yeah." Ginger snapped her gum. "She likes to hang out at The Grasshopper—it's a bar a few miles up the coast. Anyways, when she's *on a date* with someone, she likes to bring them here. It's the closest hotel that's not full of roaches and mold."

I recognized the name of the bar. Maybe Paul and this Naomi were both regulars there? I looked at Francine. "How do you know that she's a prostitute?"

Francine shrugged one rounded shoulder and snapped her gum again. "She told me. We were in the elevator one morning. She was on her way out and I was just getting off my shift. I'd seen her in here before, always with a different guy. Usually pretty dressed up. Anyways, in the elevator, she dropped an envelope and I picked it up for her and saw that it was stuffed with hundred dollar bills. I didn't say nothin' because it's none of my business, but she told me there was two grand in the envelope. She giggled about it not being bad for a night's work. Told me I was in the wrong profession."

Ginger snorted. "As if you could call what she does a *profession*."

Nick glanced down at the photo in his hands. "Had you seen the victim here before? With her?"

"Never seen him before," Francine said. "Sorry."

A sharp chirping broke into the conversation and Ginger excused herself to answer her cell phone. Francine waved to her as she went before turning back to face us. "I wish I could help, but that's all I know. When all this happened, Ginger and I were both in the laundry room. We work all our shifts together because she's my ride."

Nick nodded and pocketed the photo. "All right. Thanks for your help."

"Sure." Francine turned and followed the path her co-worker had taken and disappeared around a corner.

I shook my head, still processing how the new piece of information fit into the overall puzzle. "Well that's an interesting little tidbit."

"Very." Nick started back toward the elevator. "At least we have a name. Chief should be able to find an address."

"Unless she uses a fake name," I replied.

"Looks like I'll be going to The Grasshopper tonight," Nick said.

I laughed. "You remember when I told you that you needed to get a girlfriend? I didn't mean by the hour."

Nick rolled his eyes. "Come on. Let's get out of here. I'll swing by the station and catch Chief up, then head home to grab a few hours' sleep before I go looking for a call girl."

I elbowed him playfully. "Sounds like quite the night."

~

Nick dropped me off at the manor and I crept inside, hoping against hope that everyone would still be asleep even though it was nearly nine o'clock. Luck wasn't with me. As I walked into the kitchen, I was greeted by Mort, Bella, Adam, and Evangeline, all bright eyes and sunshine as they sat around the kitchen table. A large breakfast was laid out across the table. An old insecurity raced back to the front of my mind as I surveyed the magazine-perfect scene. Evangeline with her flawless caramel skin, exotic eyes, and literal movie-star smile sitting next to Adam, with his parents beaming across the table at them.

"Morning, Holly," Adam said after wiping his mouth on a napkin. He hopped up from his seat and came over to me. "Let's re-do these introductions, huh? Mom, Dad, this is Holly Boldt."

My cheeks warmed. "Hello, Mr. and Mrs. St. James. I'm really sorry for last night … it was all a big misunderstanding."

Mort and Bella both smiled politely. "Of course. It's very nice to finally meet you," Mort said.

"It was all a mistake." Evangeline reiterated and smiled brightly. "I mean, we've all been there, right?"

"I wouldn't say *all*," Bella muttered as Mort picked at his plate. They both kept their eyes downcast. Evangeline cringed and mouthed "sorry" to me.

Adam cleared his throat and wrapped an arm around my shoulders to steer me into the kitchen. "Let's get you a plate," he said, a little too loudly considering the table was less than three feet away.

"So, Mr. St. James—" Evangeline started, breaking the awkward silence.

"Please, call me Mort," Adam's dad corrected.

"Kill me," I whispered under my breath to Adam.

He nudged me with his elbow.

Evangeline asked Mort something related to his work and a lively conversation kicked up. Adam grabbed a plate for me but refused to release it when I reached to take it from him. His eyes locked with mine. "Where were you, Holly? I came down to wake you up for breakfast and your room was empty."

"I'm sorry. I went to make amends with Nick. My meddling cost him a client and I needed to apologize."

Adam let go of the plate. "For two hours?"

I yanked it away from him and nodded. "Don't do this, Adam. Not right now," I hissed, casting a pointed glance at the table where Evangeline was thankfully keeping Adam's parents occupied. "I said I was sorry. Drop it."

Adam rubbed at his jaw and nodded. "Fine. For now."

The look in his eyes stung me. He wasn't angry anymore. He was disappointed. For some reason, that hurt a lot more. I took the plate to the table and sat on the other side of Evangeline. The food was mostly cold, but I loaded up my plate with fruit and eggs and soggy buttered toast anyway. "Who cooked? Mrs. St. James?" I asked, expecting her to grant me permission to call her Bella.

She pursed her lips and clipped, "Adam did."

"Oh." I smiled over at Adam as he retook his seat, sandwiching Evangeline between us. "I'm surprised at the lack of peanut butter and marshmallow fluff."

Crickets. Okay, so Holly's magical comedy tour was officially not going to dig me out of this one.

Evangeline looked at me out of the corner of her eye and offered a weak smile before saying, "Well, I've gotta get to work."

Take me with you, I silently pleaded.

She patted my knee under the table and then stood, gathering her plate and coffee mug in one sweep. Her absence left a gaping hole between me and Adam. "Mort, Bella, it was very nice to meet you. And, Bella, remember to stop by the spa. I'll have Lucy refresh that manicure, no charge."

Bella beamed at Evangeline. "Wonderful! Thank you, Evie."

Evie? They were already calling her Evie?

I sagged in my seat, desperately wishing I could use the Larkspur and vanish myself to some faraway corner of the beach where no one but the seagulls could find me.

CHAPTER 15

*T*ragically, a day at the beach wasn't in the cards. After a stilted breakfast, Adam informed me that his parents wanted to take a tour of Beechwood Harbor, as they had never been before and had arrived too late the night before to really see much of anything. I hurried to dress and wished I could suck down a vial of Permasmile. Hey, it worked for Lucy. Once I was dressed, I peeked outside and frowned at the clear blue sky. At least if it started pouring down rain, I'd have a good excuse to get out of going on a walk with them.

"All right, Boots," I said, turning away from the window. "Pep talk time. Whatcha got?"

Boots yawned widely and then laid his head back on his front paws.

I frowned at him. "Well that was inspirational."

I went to the wardrobe, grabbed a scarf, and wound it around my neck. "I'll see you later. Enjoy your nap."

Halfway down the hall, I plastered on a smile and hoped I looked excited instead of deranged. I thought I'd pulled it off until Adam spotted me and asked if I'd been drinking. Mort and Bella came down the stairs a few minutes later, wearing smiles that were about as convincing as mine. Adam led the tour, pointing out the historical buildings and some of our favorite haunts as we wandered through town. I stayed beside him with my hand looped through his arm, periodically adding my own commentary.

We stopped at the bakery for a treat and then popped into Siren's Song for a pick-me-up. As we pushed through the doors of the coffee shop, I finally started to relax. Bella was starting to come around and Mort even chuckled at one of my jokes and asked for my recommendation on what to order. We took our coffees and pastries to go and continued our leisurely stroll through town.

Bella sidled up beside me. "So, Holly, Adam told us that you're from the Seattle haven. Any plans to return?"

I struggled to swallow my bite of bear claw. "Um, not exactly," I replied. I hung back a step and shot Adam a glare as Bella and Mort continued forward. What was I supposed to say?

Adam pulled me forward and flashed his parents a winning smile. "I'm afraid I've corrupted her," he started. "She likes life outside the bubble."

"Honestly, Adam. I don't understand why you are so rebellious." Bella shook her head. "I'd hoped that with your work trips into the city, you would find a nice young woman that would convince you to stay."

I looked over up at Adam, my eyes wide. *Does she not see that I'm walking right beside her?*

He winced. "Mom, we've gone over this already," he replied tersely.

"Well I want to go over it again," she snapped. "You're a shifter—"

"*Mother!*" Adam hissed, casting a glance around the streets. It was mid-morning on a weekday, so there wasn't anyone within earshot to hear Bella's declaration. "This isn't the time or the place."

Mort bristled. "Don't speak to your mother that way," he said firmly.

Bella looked over at me. "Listen, Holly, it's not anything personal."

Clearly.

"I just want Adam to have the best opportunities in life. That's all any parent wants for their children. You'll see, someday you'll have your own and it will all make sense."

I didn't know what to say. Adam had a successful business and lived life on his own terms. What more did she really want for him? If it was really about him getting married and having a family, then shouldn't she be encouraging our relationship rather than pecking at it? None of it made sense to me.

"Mom, leave Holly out of this," Adam said, putting himself between his mother and me. "I'm happy here. End of story. All right?"

He gave me a sympathetic look and I returned my attention to the pastry in my hand. But its appeal was lost. The woman actually managed to ruin my bear claw. That was an unpardonable offense in my book.

∾

"BACK SO SOON?" Nick greeted when I pushed into his office later that afternoon.

I threw myself into one of the navy blue chairs and released a long, slow sigh.

"Wow. What's up with you?"

I massaged my temples. "Adam's parents came into town early."

Nick's eyebrows arched. "Oh?"

"Yeah. They weren't supposed to be here for another week. Surprise!"

Nick chuckled. "Isn't this supposed to be a good thing? The whole 'meet the parents' routine? It's like a rite of passage."

"Passage to where? Off a cliff? Cause I'm pretty sure that's where it's going to lead."

Nick winced sympathetically. "Ouch."

I leaned forward and dropped my face into my hands. "I'm probably being paranoid, but I'm pretty sure they hate me and it hasn't even been twenty-four hours yet."

"And you thought escaping here would help? Who knows what Adam's told them about me. We both know he's not exactly a fan."

I glanced up at him. "No. He's just—"

"Holly?"

I sighed. "Okay, fine. You're right."

He chuckled again and kicked back in his seat. "Well, you wanna get out of town later tonight? I'm going up to that bar to see if I can hunt down the elusive Naomi. I haven't been able to dig up much about her, but it's pretty likely that Naomi Givens isn't her real name."

"I wish I could but Adam would go postal if I missed dinner. Let's just say breakfast was a little bit *tense*." I grimaced at the memory. "I told him I was going out to grab some soda and iced tea. If I was gone for two hours, he'd probably notice."

Nick smiled. "Fair enough. Well I'll let you know what I find out. Tomorrow I'm going to the police station to comb through some of the security footage Chief Lincoln got from the hotel."

"All right. Well if I hear anything, I'll let you know."

Nick stood from the desk and reached for his coat, and I got up too. "Good night, Holly."

"You mean good luck?" I asked, pausing at the door.

He laughed. "That too."

I left Nick's office and made my way to Thistle, the small natural foods store. They had the best root beer and were also conveniently on the route back to the manor.

While I was standing at the cash register, my cell phone rang. I blinked at the caller ID. It was Lacey. I didn't even realize she had my phone number. The cashier shot me a scowl when I answered the phone. "Hello?"

"Holly?"

I gathered my groceries quickly and haphazardly threw them into my cloth grocery sack. "Yeah?"

The background noise was so overpowering I could barely make out what she was saying. "You need to—I think —his name is—"

I waved at the cashier and she gave me a tight smile as I backed away and headed for the door. "Lacey? Where are you? I can barely hear a word you're saying!"

"Hold on a sec." The sounds muffled like she'd wrapped a hand around the microphone on her cell phone, then her voice came through loud and clear. "I'm at Raven. You need to get down here. There's a guy you need to meet. He might be able to help with the case."

I chewed on my lip, remembering my promise to Adam. I'd sworn I wouldn't get involved.

"Holly, he's got information on the dead guy."

My heart hammered. "I don't even know where the club is, Lacey."

The background noise—now a hypnotic, pulsing type of music—drowned out all other sound again for a few moments but then died off as though Lacey had moved to another room or a quiet alcove. "You know that abandoned liquor store off the highway when you take the exit for Beechwood?"

"It's there?" I asked incredulously, imagining the dusty, boarded-up shop. It was no bigger than a gas station convenience store and had been closed as long as I'd been in town. Apparently the locals hadn't taken to having a liquor store in town and had held some kind of protest until it closed down. I found it ironic, considering that it was common knowledge around town that there was more than just tea leaves inside the mugs of some of the most noted protest participants.

Lacey confirmed that I had the right place. "Yeah. Go around to the back. There's one of those garage-type doors that used to be used for deliveries. Knock twice and someone will answer. The password is gingersnaps."

I suppressed a smile. "Gingersnaps?"

Lacey sighed. "Just use it and they will let you inside. Then come find me."

"All right." I committed her instructions to memory and gave a nod. "Thanks, Lacey. I'll be there soon."

She clicked off the call and I glanced up and down the abandoned street before me. It was just starting to get dusky out, but the chilly temperatures kept people inside most nights. The local restaurants would still have patrons, but it wasn't like summertime when live music filled the streets and people sat outside at the patio tables. Everyone was inside and would rush home as soon as their meals were done.

I looked up the hill in the direction of the manor, and a hot poker of guilt stabbed at me. I knew Adam would be furious if I skipped out on dinner with his parents, but considering the way the rest of the day had gone, could he really blame me? Evangeline could take my spot at the table and carry on all kinds of charming and effortless conversation. I grimaced as the happy picture of the quartet from breakfast that morning flashed through my mind.

With a shake of my shoulders, I convinced myself it

would blow over. After all, they weren't even supposed to be in town for a few more days. Surely Adam couldn't expect me to drop everything just because they'd changed their plans. Besides that, this was no longer about me being curious or nosy. I had to protect Nick and hold up my end of the bargain with Harvey if I had any hope of getting my business back. And hey, a thirty percent slice of 100,000 dollars would be nice right about now.

With my resolve firmly locked into place, I hurried up the hill. Adam and his parents were in the living room. He and his father were watching a football game while Bella worked her way through a thick stack of magazines that I recognized from when I'd lived inside the haven system. They were the supernatural equivalent of the gossip rags that humans stock at the check-out lanes of grocery stores. All eyes turned to me when I walked in.

Adam smiled at me. "Hey, gorgeous."

"Hey there! I got some stuff from Thistle. For dinner."

Adam pushed up from the couch as his parents returned their attention to their own interests. "Let me help you," he said, reaching to take the single bag from my hands.

We went into the kitchen and Adam started unpacking the groceries. He closed the fridge and turned to face me. "Listen, Holls, about earlier—"

I held up a hand. "It's fine, Adam. I get it. I'm not what they were expecting."

"No, no," he insisted, rushing forward to grab my arms. He held me steady, his eyes wide with concern. "That's not it. I swear, Holly. This isn't about you at all. I'm the one they're disappointed with."

I arched an eyebrow at him. "It sure doesn't feel that way. Were you not listening when your mother went on for twenty minutes about how ambitious you've always been and how hard you've worked to build your business? I mean, I'm impressed too, but that was borderline nauseating."

Adam smiled even as he flicked his eyes toward the ceiling in a subtle roll. "Believe me, I heard it all. You just gotta trust me on this one. They want me to move back to the haven, stop working for humans, and basically be a good little shifter."

"If that's what they're upset about, then why does it feel like they hate me?"

Adam ran his hands up and down my arms. "They don't hate you, gorgeous. They'll only be satisfied when I find some woman who wants to drag me back to the haven and can convince me to continue the family name by passing it down to a whole house full of little Adams."

My lips quirked into a smile. "Which, as a concept, terrifies me. I can barely keep up with one full-grown Adam."

He laughed softly and pulled me into his arms. I rested my head against his solid chest and took a deep breath. "Promise me you'll give it another chance, Holly? I'll talk to them. I'll fix this."

I sighed. "I don't think this is something you can fix, Adam. They're not going to change their minds or lower their expectations for you."

"Well they're going to have to, because I have no intention of going back to a haven anytime soon." He looked down into my eyes and traced a finger down the side of my face. "Especially not without you."

"Good thing you didn't tell them about the whole banishment thing then, huh?"

Adam cringed. "Yeah …"

"Well why don't you have dinner with them solo tonight. Maybe you guys can work through some of these *issues* and we can all have a do-over dinner tomorrow night when I get off work."

Adam looked ready to object, but I cocked my head, giving him full-on puppy eyes, and he swallowed whatever argument he'd been ready to make. "All right. What about you though? What are you gonna do for dinner?"

I patted his chest and gave him a sly wink. "Don't you worry about me, Mr. St. James."

He smiled. "I thought that was part of my boyfriend job description?"

I laughed and popped up on my toes to press a quick kiss to his lips. "I'll be good. I promise. Lacey called a little while ago. I'll go meet her."

Adam gave me a skeptical frown but before he could prod for more information, his dad called for him from the other room, following a series of whoops. He turned back to me. "I'll see you later?"

"Yeah. Of course."

He kissed my forehead before letting me go, and when he paused at the kitchen door, a fuzzy orange paw appeared in the crack. With a smile, he pushed the door open wide enough for Boots to wiggle the rest of himself into the kitchen. "Have fun with Lacey."

"Bet you'd never thought you'd say something like that, huh?"

He chuckled and waved to me and then left me alone in the kitchen.

Once alone, I leaned into the counter and sucked in a deep breath. Boots rammed into my shins and I bent down to pet him on the head. "Don't worry, Bootsie. I wouldn't dream of leaving without making sure you were well fed first."

He meowed and I laughed to myself on the way to his food cupboard. "It's nice to know that some things never change, Bootsie."

CHAPTER 16

I followed Lacey's instructions and, with a little help from the Larkspur, managed to arrive at the abandoned liquor store roughly twenty minutes after her phone call. I expected her to huff and fuss about my tardiness all the same, but the odds were good that whoever it was she wanted me to meet was still within her sights. A gust of wind kicked up as I walked around to the loading door at the back of the building.

I tugged the collar of my coat up around my neck and wondered what the dress code would be on the other side of the door. Lacey hadn't said anything—and would likely comment on my wardrobe choices no matter what I wore— but I wondered if I should have changed into something a little less American Eagle and a little more Saks Fifth Avenue. After all, vamps like glamour. It was part of their claim to fame: utterly terrifying but impossibly chic.

The large garage-style door was shut tight and, without a clear window or knob, I wasn't sure where to knock. I delivered two hard raps to the center of the door, thankful for the thick gloves on my hands that protected me from the biting chill of the metal sheet. When a moment of silence passed, a swarm of butterflies escaped and rocketed around my stomach as I looked around. Was I in the wrong place? I dismissed the theory. This was the only abandoned liquor store off the highway. Lacey's instructions had been too specific for me to have made a mistake. As I was debating my next move, a bright flood light burst on from above the door. I shielded my eyes against the sudden harsh light.

"Password?" a deep voice demanded.

I jumped and spun around to find myself squared off with a tall, broad-shouldered vampire who looked like he'd spent the night sucking on a lemon. "Um—gingersnaps?"

The vampire blinked coolly as he sized me up. "Who're you here with?"

A chill ran down my spine. "I'm not. It's just me."

He crossed his arms and I tried not to stare at his thickly muscled his arms, each of which was roughly the size of a small tree trunk. Yeah ... he could snap me in half without even trying. I didn't know much about this elusive Raven club, but they had excellent taste in bouncers.

I mustered up every ounce of courage I had and conjured a simple orb of light. I bounced it casually between my hands and looked him in the eye. "I gave you the password. You gonna let me in or not?"

After a long moment, he took a step to the side and let me in through a door that hadn't been visible before. I blinked at its sudden appearance, automatically analyzing what kind of charm had been applied to make the door invisible. The bouncer issued a warning as he moved aside to let me through. "Stay out of trouble, *witch*."

I smothered the light in my palms. "Noted," I muttered, snaking past without brushing up against him.

As I hurried down the hallway, my eyes adjusted to the dim lighting. A closer look revealed a space that was much larger than it should have been, considering the limits of the physical building. Some pretty serious magic had been invested in the creation of the sprawling club. How had this place existed under my nose all this time without even so much as a whisper of it reaching my ears? After all, up until Harvey torpedoed my business, I'd been right in the center of the local supernatural population. I couldn't believe it had never come up in conversation. I ached at the thought of how many potential customers lurked in the corners of the large room. I'd missed out on all of them.

The club was painted a deep shade of red and illuminated with soft, glowing lights that floated and moved like fairies were skating through the air overhead. A large dance floor dominated most of the room, and from my spot along the wall, I watched the cluster of dancers as they swayed together to the same hypnotic beats I'd heard while on the phone with Lacey.

Along the opposite wall, a bar spanned the length of the room, lined with twenty-plus bar stools floating in mid-air. I watched as a tall, lanky woman hopped daintily onto one of the stools and marveled as it automatically adjusted to account for her size, holding her at exactly the right height. A dark-skinned bartender with a dazzling smile approached the woman and, moments later, handed her a goblet of deep red liquid. The woman laughed at something he said as he leaned in to serve it to her.

Everything was mesmerizing, but I forced myself to snap out of it and start my search for Lacey. I was only here to get ahead in the case, not to drink and dance. That is, assuming they even had something other than six different types of synthetic blood on tap. I scanned the dance floor, trying to pick out her familiar face as the lights above moved and swayed.

"Holly!"

I twisted in the direction of the sound of my name and found Lacey rushing at me. As expected, she was decked out in a skin-tight black dress that highlighted her luminescent skin and made her long blonde hair stand out like creamy satin in contrast. She slowed her pace as she neared and my cheeks went red as she scanned my own outfit. "That's what you decided to wear?" she hissed in a low voice. Her ski-slope nose wrinkled as she gave me another once-over before snaking her arm through mine and dragging me out of the entryway.

"I didn't have time to change," I protested, yanking my arm free from hers.

"Weren't you with Adam's parents earlier?"

"Yeah. So?"

She scoffed and rolled her eyes. "Honestly, Holly. I should give you classes."

We walked as she lectured me on my fashion sense until we reached a booth hidden in shadows in the corner of the club. My lips locked together as I found myself staring into a pair of eyes so dark they looked black. Lacey slid into the booth and snapped her wrist for me to sit beside her. The man in the booth appraised me with a suave, secretive smile and he inclined his head. "Ms. Boldt?"

I laced my hands together under the table. There was something unnerving about the vampire sitting across from me. He was stunning; almost beautiful. His features were perfectly sculpted and his dark hair and eyes lent him an air of mystery and danger. "Yes. And you are?"

He smiled wide enough that the sharp tips of his fangs peeked out and a shiver ran down my spine. "Dread."

"Is that your name of more of a general warning?"

Lacey tossed her blonde hair over her shoulder, apparently unaffected by the man across from us. "Dread is a member of the Molder House. He's Greyson Molder's second."

I nodded, like I had any idea what that meant. "Lacey said you have information on Paul Banks' murder," I said, wanting to get to the meat of the conversation so I could scramble away from Dread's intense stare.

Dread leaned back in his seat and casually spun the crystal glass on the table in front of him. "That depends."

"On?" My eyebrows furrowed together. "I'm not sure I follow."

Dread took a maddeningly slow sip of his faux blood cocktail before leaning in. He dropped his voice another octave lower, "Ms. Boldt, I don't know what you know about this *situation*, but you've obviously gotten in deep enough for it to have led you here. And your instincts, or whatever led you to this point, were right. I do indeed know who killed Paul."

"You do?" I whispered.

Dread grinned and nodded slowly. "I do. But information like that doesn't come cheap, Ms. Boldt."

I glanced at Lacey and she shifted in her seat, refusing to make eye contact with me. What was going on here? My heart slammed in my chest and my stomach caved in on itself. "What would the price be, Mr. Dread?" I gulped. I was afraid of the answer; human blood was a delicacy that bordered on addiction for many vampires.

Dread laughed and despite, his warm and polished exterior, the sound was cold and chilling. "I assure you, it's not what you're thinking, Ms. Boldt. Blood is a cheap commodity that can be had just by walking out this door and charming the first person that attracts me."

Well, that was unsettling.

At least he didn't want mine. A sigh of relief hitched in

my throat as Dread's eyes narrowed and locked with mine. "I need a favor."

"What do you need from me?" I asked, giving Lacey another sideways glance. She wouldn't have set me up, but maybe she hadn't been aware there would be something expected of me.

"You're still working with that SPA agent, right?"

I swallowed hard. How did he know about Harvey? That was all supposed to be a secret. Nobody should have known about my involvement with him, not even that he was my assigned agent.

Dread smiled and took another long sip, happy to let me squirm a moment longer. He tutted, then said, "Come on, Ms. Boldt. We both want the same things here. Don't be shy." He set down his crystal glass and turned the stem in his fingers. His mesmerizing gaze never dropped from mine. "I want the SPA out of town and from what I know of your history, you must want the same thing. Come on—tell me I'm wrong."

I looked at Lacey and she stared at the table.

"Ms. Vaughn didn't rat you out," Dread interjected, glancing at Lacey. "If that's what you're worried about. The Molder House doesn't concern themselves with *underlings* but there are certain names we listen for. Boldt is one of them."

"Underlings?" I snarled. Magic pooled in my palms, hot and fast.

Dread merely shrugged. "If you want the name of Paul's murderer, then I need you to go along with my plan and not share the source of this information with the SPA. We would like the Vampire Council to handle this situation."

"So it *was* a vampire that killed Paul? What about Naomi Givens?"

Dread didn't blink. He held my gaze for a long moment before asking, "Do we have a deal, Ms. Boldt?"

I couldn't lie to a vampire. That was not a bridge I wanted to burn. Vampires were ruthless and didn't take kindly to those who double-crossed them. If I agreed to his terms, then I would be backing out of my deal with Harvey. If I did that, I'd never have a chance to get my potion business back.

I pushed up from the table. "I'm sorry to have wasted your time, Mr. Dread, but I can't agree to those terms."

"Holly—" Lacey said, reaching for me.

I whipped around at the touch of her hands. "Lacey, how could you think I'd agree to this? You know that I can't afford trouble with the SPA. I can't trust some underground council to bring justice for Paul and probably for Naomi too, wherever she is."

Dread looked completely unruffled by the entire turn of events. It apparently didn't matter to him whether or not the murder went unsolved forever—a fact that only incensed me further. "Have it your way, Ms. Boldt. But if the killer isn't stopped, this won't be the only body you're going to have on your hands. You really want that on your conscience?"

I stopped at the end of the table and slammed my hands to the table. Bolts of magic bounced against the surface of the wood with a loud crack and I could feel eyeballs on me. I dropped my voice low, "I would say the same to you, but we both know your kind don't have souls. And I'm pretty sure that's a prerequisite to having a conscious."

"Holly!" Lacey snapped.

I glanced at her. "I'm sorry, Lacey, but I'm not going to be blackmailed by this … this …"

"Monster?" Dread offered with a sneer.

"If the fangs fit …"

He smirked, then carelessly shrugged a shoulder. "Hey, I tried to help."

"Yourself, maybe."

Lacey scoffed and pushed up from her own seat. "This is the last time I get involved in one of your little Nancy Drew capers, Holly." She stalked off in a huff.

Dread chuckled. "Making friends all over town tonight, huh Boldt?"

I glared at him and pushed off the table. "I don't need your information to pin this on one of your *esteemed* members. I have Georgia and I have the Thraxis medallion. I'll trust the SPA will deal with you. A few drops of their highest level truth serum will have you spilling your guts in front of the council like that—" I snapped my fingers inches from his face.

Dread struck like a viper and grabbed my wrist in a vice-like clench. "What do you know about the Thraxis?" he growled.

I yanked my arm but his grip help tight. "Let go of me and I'll repeat myself. Then I'm out of here or your friends are gonna get a little fireworks show," I said, keeping my own voice low as I held up my opposite hand to reveal the pool of bright orange magic.

He released me and asked again, "What do you know about the Thraxis?"

"I know where it is and I'm pretty sure I can get more information out of its current owner than I could ever have gotten out of you."

Dread's smirk was gone, leaving his expression icy and stern. "Where is it? Who has it?"

I took a half step back, surprised by his sudden interest. "Why? What do you want with it?"

"It's a House heirloom and it's missing. It's my duty, as a Molder, to retrieve it."

Apparently a case of the right hand not knowing what the left was doing. Greyson Molder was the last one in possession of the medallion, and he'd given it to his paramour. I struggled to keep from smiling as I leaned in and said, "Tell me who killed Paul and I'll tell you who has the necklace."

Dread frowned. "Greyson Molder killed Paul Banks."

The information rattled through my system. The satisfaction of playing the game, and winning, dissipated in light of Dread's answer. The smile slid off my face as I realized the ramifications of what I'd just been told.

Dread continued flatly, "They were doing some business dealings together. I don't know all the details. But a couple of weeks ago, things went south. Greyson killed him."

I tried to keep my face from revealing my surprise. "What about Naomi?"

Dread smiled coldly. "She's one of us. She was in on it from the beginning. She lured Banks to that hotel and Greyson was already waiting in the room."

I cringed. It was too cruel to fathom.

"Now, *witch*, tell me where the medallion is."

"You'll have to ask your boss about that," I said before storming away from the table. To my surprise, Dread didn't follow.

I didn't bother looking for Lacey. I hurried for the exit and pushed out, grateful for the first sharp breath of frost-laced air. Someone was lying and if the web of deceit wasn't untangled soon, there was more than just one life on the line.

CHAPTER 17

*W*hen I arrived back at the manor, things quickly shifted gears. Evangeline greeted me at the door, her arm linked with a man who looked to be a few years older than she was. He had rosy cheeks, sandy blonde hair, and megawatt smile. She beamed and said, "Holly, this is Teddy."

"Teddy? Oh, right!" I slapped my hand over my face and shook my head. The lawyer. "I'm sorry. Long night."

"That's all right," Teddy said, flashing what I guessed was his signature smile. He offered me a hand and I shook it. "It's nice to meet you, Holly. Evangeline said you needed some help with a Haven Council issue?"

I nodded and gave Evangeline a distracted smile. "That's right. Umm, I forgot you were coming in tonight. I really appreciate you being here but my mind is a little full right now."

Evangeline patted Teddy on the arm and smiled up at him. "That's all right, Holly. We were actually going to get something for dinner and catch up. But I wanted you guys to meet first. Are you free tomorrow so you two can meet up?"

"Um, I work until three and then I promised Adam we'd have dinner with his parents," I replied, glancing past Evangeline's shoulder to see if Adam was in earshot. The manor had plenty of room for all of us to sprawl out, but was quiet enough that I concluded Adam and his parents were still out to dinner. He was likely exposing them to the wonders of McNally's. "But let's say four o'clock. Would that work?"

Teddy smiled. "Of course, Ms. Boldt."

"Oh, please, call me Holly."

"All right, Holly. We'll meet then and figure out a plan of attack."

I nodded. "Thank you. You have no idea how much I appreciate it."

Evangeline tugged on Teddy's arm, guiding him toward the open door, and they waved before ducking out into the night. I shut the door behind them and went down the hall to my room.

Boots was curled up in a tight ball in the center of my bed, snoring softly. I didn't even stop to kick out of my shoes before flopping down beside his warm body. He stirred slightly and I laid a hand over his back and lulled him back to sleep. In the silence, I let my mind unwind, spiraling through all the thoughts and theories and worries that I'd shoved to the back. But the longer I drifted, the more confused I became.

I heaved a sigh and Boots stirred. "Sorry buddy."

Before he woke up completely, I pushed up into a sitting position and angled my legs off the side of the bed. I kicked out of my boots and then padded to the wardrobe against the opposite wall to find a pair of fuzzy pajamas. I needed warm clothes, soothing tea, and a Lemon Cloud.

As I was changing, I brushed my fingers over the Larkspur around my neck and decided it couldn't hurt to brain storm with my Great-Grandmother Honeysuckle before going to the kitchen. After all, she was a vast source of information and had proven helpful in the two prior cases I'd wound up tangled in.

I stroked the smooth metal and popped the clasp at the side. The locket opened and revealed a semi-fogged mirror. I waited as the edges cleared and revealed Grandmother Honeysuckle, looking regal as ever with her perfectly coiffed hair and pressed dress. I waited for the rest of the mirrored surface to clear. "Grandmother Honeysuckle?"

She blinked slowly and I wondered if she'd been asleep, if that was even possible. After a moment, she jolted forward and smiled. "Oh, hello there, Harvest!"

I bit back a groan. "Holly. Grandmother, my name is *Holly*."

"Holly? Hmm. Are you sure, dear?"

"I'm relatively confident. Yes."

She considered me for another moment and then flapped a hand. "In any case, how are you, dear? Found a nice young wizard to settle down with?"

I sighed and shook my head, wondering why I'd thought it was a good idea to summon her in the first place. "Still looking," I said, not wanting to open that box again. "In the meantime, Grandmother Honeysuckle, I need your help with something."

"Of course, Harvest."

My jaw flexed. "Holly."

"What about it, dear? It's very good in salves and memory potions."

"I—no—that's—" I sputtered. "Never mind."

Grandmother Honeysuckle frowned, as though I were the one exhausting her. "Well then what is it, dear?"

"When you made the Larkspur and forged your spirit to it, did you happen to look into any other types of magically enhanced jewelry? I mean where did the idea come from?"

"Hmm. That's a good question," she replied, smoothing her fingers over her hair. "I was traveling and met a druid who had locked his spirit inside of a tree planted beside the grave of his true love. He could live his life, but a piece of him remained behind. It got me thinking that it was a good way to go on beyond this life, even when the rest of me is in the Otherworld."

"Are there other necklaces like the Larkspur then?"

She shook her head. "Not that I know of. I was something of a pioneer," she replied, puffing her chest out slightly like a preening peacock.

"Have you heard of a medallion with the Thraxis engraved on its face?"

Grandmother Honeysuckle's brow wrinkled. "You mean that gaudy Molder House bauble?"

I nodded, although I didn't agree with her *gaudy* assessment. It was actually a quite elegant piece. "Yes."

She frowned. "Sullivan Molder was the one who commissioned the piece. Once forged, he kidnapped a witch and forced her to enchant the necklace."

"What did they want it to do?"

"Allow them to go into the sunlight, of course. That's what *all* vampires want, dear. They envy those of us who can live in the light."

"Oh." I blinked a few times. The thought had never occurred to me. In all of my time living at the manor I'd never once heard Lacey complain about her odd schedule. And it wasn't that she was too shy to say anything. No, complaining and pitching dramatic woe-is-me parties were a semi-regular occurrence for the vampiress. "So the Thraxis can do that?"

Grandmother Honeysuckle shook her head. "Not as far as I know. Before she died, the witch, cursed the wearer of the necklace. Any vampire that wears it will come down with a terrible disease that eventually sends them back to the dust where they belong. They never made another one after the original killed Sullivan."

I'd apparently missed this lesson back in my academy days. "What would happen if a human wore the necklace?"

Honeysuckle reared back. "Why on earth would a human wear such a thing?"

"Let's say they found it at a flea market."

"A *what* market?"

"Flea?"

"Why in the name of the goddess would there be a market to purchase fleas? Back in my day you got those for free at nearly every market."

"It's uh—just an expression." I sighed. Right. Seven-generation age gap. Not to mention, granny didn't exactly have access to the internet. Or an encyclopedia for that matter. "What do you think would happen? Would the human get sick too?"

Grandmother Honeysuckle shook her head. "I don't think so. But then, I don't know for sure what would happen."

The mirror faded and Grandmother Honeysuckle's image started to blur at the edges. "Looks like it's time for me to go, Holly. Do visit again soon, dear. I'll give you my secret tips on flirting so you can snag a nice young wizard."

She winked at me and then was gone.

I closed the locket and flopped back on the bed. "That was less than helpful," I said to Boots' sleeping form. The last time I'd seen Georgia, she'd shown no signs of disease. She hadn't even sniffled or coughed. Maybe the Thraxis didn't affect humans. But it still didn't explain why Greyson Molder had given it to her in the first place. Maybe he treated it like any other piece of jewelry. He couldn't wear it and neither could any other members of the Molder House, so what difference did it make if he gave it to his girlfriend? He could take it back once he'd turned her and explain it was dangerous. The only thing that still didn't make sense was why Dread had lit up like a string of Christmas lights when I'd mentioned it, and not in a good way. Why did he want it? He couldn't wear it. And if it was really such a meaningless thing, a trinket, then why hadn't Greyson told his second who was in possession of it?

The thoughts were still rolling through my mind as I reached for a Lemon Cloud and flicked on the nightly Witch Wire to distract myself.

≈

BEFORE CLOCKING in for my shift at Siren's Song the following morning, I stopped by Nick's office to see if he'd heard anything from Georgia. She might have fired him from the case, but surely she'd still call him if something weird was going on. Nick was wearing the same suit he'd had on the day before and from the dark circles under his eyes, it was obvious he hadn't gone home for a good night's sleep. He barely glanced up when I walked into the office. "Rough night?" I asked, sinking into the seat across from him.

He smiled, or at least attempted to. "It was a late night. But a productive one."

"Oh? Another stakeout money shot?"

He shook his head. "Nope. Got a confession. The Banks murder case is closed."

"What?" My heart screeched to a halt. "What are you talking about? A confession? Who? When? What happened?"

Nick chuckled and held up both hands. "Way too tired for twenty questions, Holls."

"Last thing I knew, you were going to the bar the hotel maids mentioned. Now this? I think I need at least ten questions."

"Five."

"Seven."

"Six. Final offer," Nick smiled tiredly.

I smiled. "Deal."

Nick chuckled and scrubbed a hand down his face. "I did go to the bar. Naomi wasn't there. No one had seen her for a few days. One of the regulars knew where she lived, so I went over to pay her a visit. When I got there, I found her husband, Gus. We got to talking. He seemed really disoriented and out of it. I asked where Naomi was and he said he hadn't seen her in days. I showed him a picture of Paul and —" Nick paused and shook his head.

"And?" I prompted, every nerve on red alert.

"And before I knew it, he was confessing. To everything. He said he knew what Naomi did on the side and never said anything, but that night, as she was leaving the house, he commented on her choice of dress and they got into a big fight. Shouting, screaming, whole neighborhood heard it. Ugly. He said he followed her to the bar, then to the hotel. He waited until they were in the room and then he went up and continued the fight. At one point it got physical and he ended up killing Paul. Naomi got scared and ran off before he could stop her."

I heard every word of Nick's story, but none of the words fit together. They were like mismatched puzzle pieces. Naomi's husband confessed to the murder? But why? He didn't do it. Unless Dread was wrong. Maybe Greyson was just talking it up, taking credit for the murder to give him more cred as the leader of the Molder House.

I wrung my hands together in my lap, twisting my fingers as the thoughts and theories churned in my mind.

"I'm tellin' ya, Holls. It was the weirdest experience ever. I mean, I've heard that a guilty conscious can make someone do something crazy, but just blabbing a murder confession like that? It was crazy."

"I'll bet," I said, my mind going a mile a minute. "So this Gus, he doesn't have any idea where Naomi is now? She ran away from the home they share and hasn't been back since? No calls or anything?"

Nick shook his head. "That's what I was up all night trying to figure out. Gus was taken into police custody and I was too wired to go home and sleep. Gus gave me her cell phone before he was hauled off, so I was trying to get a clue where she might be. I'll probably go home and crash for a few hours and then try the bar again tonight. See if she circles back to her regular spot."

"You really think she would go back and risk Gus finding her? She won't know he's in custody. Right?"

"I suppose not." Nick frowned. "Well it's worth a shot. I couldn't find any other leads."

I cocked my head. "How did he seem? Was he agitated or angry when he was talking to you?"

Nick shook his head. "Not at all. That was part of the reason it felt so odd. He was calm. Almost monotone."

A new theory came to life in the pit of my stomach. "Are you sure he doesn't have an alibi of some kind? Maybe he was just confused."

Nick frowned at me, his eyebrows knitting together. "He did it, Holly. He murdered Paul Banks because he was sleeping with his wife. It's pretty open and shut. No one is going to do a lot of digging now that he's confessed."

I shook my head. "Something feels off."

Nick sighed impatiently. "Off how? He had motive, opportunity, and gave a full, willing confession. What more could you possibly want, Holly? This is a dream case. No loose ends, shaky evidence, or question marks."

With a heavy sigh of my own, I pushed up from seat and pocketed my hands. "You're right. I'm sorry."

Nick tilted his head as he considered me. "You okay, Holls?"

I nodded. "Yeah. Congrats on cracking another case, Nick. I'm sure Chief Lincoln is relieved."

"Yeah. As long as he doesn't recant, we should be in the clear. If we're lucky, he'll take a plea deal and spare us all the headache of a trial."

"Right." I started for the door. "I gotta get over to work. See you later?"

He grinned and nodded. "Nap first. Then I'll come get my second wind in a cardboard cup."

"Solid plan." I smiled. "See you later, Nick."

ick came into Siren's Song just as the last group of customers from the lunch rush was heading for the door. He'd changed into a pair of jeans and sneakers and a dark blue waterproof jacket. "Feeling better, Sleeping Beauty?" I teased as he strolled up to the counter.

He flashed a wide smile. "I'm not sure if it was the nap or the fat check that's got me in a better mood."

My eyebrows shot up. "You got it already?"

"Yes, ma'am."

"Wow. What did Georgia say?"

"Not much, really." Nick shrugged. "I think she's relieved it's over so soon."

"So she wasn't upset that you're the one getting the reward money? After everything that happened?"

"I don't think so." He glanced down into the front case to pick something for lunch. "I'll do the tuna wrap and as many white chocolate chip cookies as you have in stock."

I laughed and started putting together his order. "Mr. Big Spender, huh?"

"You know it." He chuckled and reached for his wallet. "Guess I'll settle out my tab."

I laughed and boxed up the cookies. "Yeah, don't make me send the dogs after you."

As I was punching in his order and the items from his running tab, Cassie appeared from the back room. "Hey, Nick. How are you?"

Nick inclined his head in her direction in a respectful nod. "Doing good. I'm sure Chief told you we got our guy."

Cassie leaned against the front counter and nodded. "Yeah. He stopped in for lunch and told me the good news."

"He did?" I asked, looking up from the register.

"Briefly. Just long enough to get a sandwich and coffee. He's been working some long days since that man was murdered." Cassie twirled the end of her long braid around her fingers. "He won't really talk about it much but from what I've gathered, it was a pretty chilling case. I'm glad it's over."

Nick murmured in agreement.

"Fifty-six fifty," I told Nick.

He let out a low whistle. "Man, I need to cut back on my mocha consumption."

Cassie and I both laughed. "Yeah," she scoffed. "Like that's gonna happen. We all know you're a hopeless addict."

Nick chuckled and handed over a stack of bills. "Keep the change."

"Thanks." I made the correct change and slipped the extra bills and change into the tip jar on the counter beside the register before slamming the drawer shut with a pop of my hip. "What's the plan now that you got your guy? Any new cases?"

"Chief Lincoln wants me to keep trying to track down Naomi. After that ... I don't know."

Cassie pushed off the counter. "Well I know that Phillip

149

wants to hire someone to set up a security system here at the shop. Maybe I could send him your information?" she offered with a slight shrug.

Nick smiled at her. "Thanks, Cass, but security systems aren't exactly my specialty. If things get really boring, I'll just have to reopen my side business."

"Your ghost tours?" Cassie asked with a giggle.

Nick frowned at her. "What's so funny about that?"

She stifled her laugh and waved a hand at him. "Nothing. I think it sounds like fun. Sign me up for your first one."

Nick glanced at me. "What about you, Holls? You wanna go hunt some ghosts?"

If only he knew.

"Ya know, I think I'm good. I'm not sure I believe in all that hocus-pocus stuff," I said, miraculously managing to keep a straight face.

Nick picked up his box of goodies and headed for the door. "See you ladies later."

"Bye, Nick," we both called after him.

When he was gone, Cassie started giggling again. "He really is an odd duck, isn't he?"

"He is. But that's all right. Keeps things interesting around here."

She agreed and I followed her to the back room where she'd been working on checking in an order from the bakery. I leaned against the wall and smiled at the pink bakery boxes. "Any chance there's something damaged?" I asked, my stomach seconding my question with a loud rumble.

Cassie laughed softly. "There's a blueberry muffin over there that I already dug into. Help yourself."

I reached for the muffin she'd indicated and broke off a piece. "How are things going here? I feel like I went from living here to being totally out of the loop."

Cassie glanced up at me from over the top of her clipboard. "I know. I've missed having you around."

My heart twisted. "I miss you too, Cass."

"Things are good though," she said with a smile. "Paisley is here full time and Kirra's been pulling more hours because she has a lighter school load this quarter. I hired someone to help my dad during the day when I'm here at work."

"You did? Oh, Cass, that's wonderful!"

She gave me a watery smile. "It is. It's so nice to know that he's not lonely anymore, and Quinn is wonderful. She's in her mid-forties and they get along great. She watches TV with him, helps him cook and does some light cleaning. My dad really likes her too, even though they argue about baseball all day."

I laughed. "Sounds perfect. And things with Chief are good?"

Cassie's cheeks flushed slightly and I smiled. It was adorable how she still got flustered over him even though they'd been together for quite a few months. "He's great. I'm so glad I gave him a second chance."

I hopped up on the table and popped another bite of muffin into my mouth. "Do you ever wonder what would have happened if you'd said yes to him back in high school? Like what would have happened if you'd gone to the prom together?"

Cassie laughed. "That's funny. We were actually talking about that not too long ago. He asked what I would say if he asked me to the prom now. He was just joking, obviously, but it got us talking. I don't know for sure what would have happened, but I think that where we ended up is pretty great, so who am I to say I wished we'd done things differently?"

"I'm really happy for you, Cass."

"Thanks, Holly." She smiled up at me and paused her

counting. "What about you and Adam? Still worried about his parents coming into town?"

I tried not to laugh. Or was it cry? "They actually surprised us both and came into town early."

"Oh?"

"Yeah. It's been … interesting." I couldn't fill Cassie in on the oh-so-fantastic details. Like the part where the first time they saw me I was wearing handcuffs. Or that they're star-struck by my gorgeous roommate, who's a former paranormal soap star. Or that they're going to resent me unless I can somehow convince Adam to move back to the haven system—which would be tricky, seeing as how I'm not even allowed to visit.

Cassie cocked her head. "How so?"

I dragged in a sigh and polished off the rest of the blueberry muffin. Comfort food was required if we were gonna talk about Adam's parents. I started eyeballing a croissant in case I needed backup. "They seem to want a certain *type* for Adam and unfortunately I don't think I fit the mold."

Cassie frowned. "Like what? You're gorgeous, smart, ambitious, and you make their son very happy. What more could they possibly want?"

"Thanks, Cass." I pushed my hair back from my face. "I think they want him to be with someone who wants to get married, have kids, and be more of a homemaker, I guess. They don't seem to appreciate my entrepreneurial spirit and the fact that I'm not pushing Adam to move to a big city and expand his business. Oh, and his mom's wardrobe puts mine to shame."

Cassie wrinkled her nose. "Ugh. I'm sorry, Holly. That doesn't sound like fun. How long will they be in town?"

"Another week I think."

"Ouch."

I sighed deeply. "It'll be fine. Adam doesn't seem to be

taking it all that seriously. It could be worse. He could be one of those mama's boys who does whatever his mom wants. Adam is more duck and water with all of this."

"Yeah, he's not exactly the type to be swayed, is he?"

I smiled. "Not at all."

The bell at the front door jingled and I hopped off the table to go help the incoming customers.

$\approx$

WHEN MY SHIFT WAS OVER, Cassie was on her way out for the day as well. We parted ways out front when Chief Lincoln pulled up in his sedan to pick her up. I smiled as he scrambled to get out of the car and hurried around to open the passenger door in time for her to slide into the seat. We waved to each other and I watched as they drove off into the night.

My conversation with Cassie played back through my mind as I hoofed it back up to the manor. For Cassie, whether she wanted to admit it or not, getting engaged to Chief Lincoln and settling down would be a dream come true. I was happy for her and hoped she got a big, sparkly ring, but while I was thinking about it, I had to admit to myself that I didn't want that from Adam. We were in a completely different place, and after spending time with his parents, I wondered if I'd ever be able to live up to their expectations—or his. We hadn't talked about it, but while Adam might not want to move back to the havens anytime soon, he hadn't denied wanting to settle down and start a family. The problem was that I didn't know if that was what I wanted.

Evangeline and Teddy were waiting for me in the living room when I got back to the manor. When I joined them after kicking out of my shoes and saying hello to Boots, I noticed that they were sitting so close together they were practically sharing a couch cushion. I took the loveseat adjacent to them and Teddy started the meeting. "So tell me, Holly, what is it that you're hoping to accomplish with the hearing?"

"All I've ever wanted is to get my potions master license so I can legally sell my custom potions, both here in the human world and inside the havens."

Beside Teddy, a pen hovered over a green notepad and moved of its own accord as I spoke. He followed my gaze and offered a quick smile. "I hope you don't mind. I find I need a little help keeping notes."

I nodded. "Right. Not a problem."

Teddy clasped his hands together and leaned forward. "I'll shoot straight with you, Holly. I've poked around your record and can already tell you it's going to be a hard road, but I think we have a shot. As you know, the Haven Council can be a bit *biased*. But that's fine. We know what we're walking into and we will fight hard to keep the focus on you and your business and keep the mess with Gabriel out of the conversation."

"Trust me, I'm all for that. He has nothing to do with this, so I don't see the point in discussing him."

Teddy nodded. "Good."

"Tell him about Harvey," Evangeline interjected.

"Oh! Right. Harvey Colepepper is my SPA case worker and he's agreed to testify on my behalf," I explained to Teddy. There was no reason to point out that he would only do so if and when we solved the mess with the vampires. And now that a human had confessed to the crime, I wasn't sure where that left things with Harvey's investigation. I decided staying positive was the best course of action.

Teddy nodded, excited. "That's great! That will help a lot. Listen, I'm going back to the LA haven tomorrow, but I'll be in touch and start filing paperwork for a hearing on your behalf. We should be able to get before the Council within a few months' time."

"Great! Thank you so much," I said, glancing at both of them in turn.

A voice sounded from the arched entry to the foyer. "Knock, knock."

Adam was wearing jeans and his signature leather jacket. "Holly, you ready to go?" he asked. "We were thinking McNally's would be a good choice. They're having that five-bean stew tonight that you like."

"Sure," I replied, smiling at him even as my heartbeat ratcheted into overdrive. "I'll be right there."

"Okay, grab your coat." He glanced at Evangeline, Teddy, and then back at me before turning to go back down the hall.

"I should get going. Is there anything else you need from me?"

Teddy shook his head. "Not right now. Like I said, I'll get in touch once I'm back at my office."

"Okay," I replied, nodding. "I feel bad that you came all this way just for that …"

Teddy smiled over at Evangeline. "Don't worry about it, Holly. The trip was more than worth it."

"Right." I pushed up from the couch, suddenly feeling like an awkward third wheel. As much as I was dreading the dinner that lay ahead, it seemed a better option than watching Teddy and Evangeline go gaga over each other. "Have a safe trip back."

"Night, Holly!" Evangeline called after me as I slipped from the room.

CHAPTER 19

cNally's was unusually busy when we arrived and we ended up waiting a handful of minutes for a table to open up. We awkwardly hung back by the front door, all four of us shifting from one foot to the other and avoiding eye contact. A thick tension loomed over our heads but no one wanted to make the first move. Adam kept glancing at me, as though I was somehow supposed to conjure up something to say. *Sorry pal, magic doesn't work like that.*

After what felt like an hour but was probably closer to five minutes, a waitress came to take us to a table in the back. She passed out menus with a smile and sashayed away to get our drinks while we decided what we wanted to eat. I watched her go and wished I could follow. I'd rather be elbow-deep in dirty dishes than sitting across from Mort and Bella with nothing to say, pretending that I hadn't seen the McNally's menu a thousand and one times before.

"So, Mom, Dad, what were your thoughts for Yule dinner?" Adam asked when the silence became deafening.

Bella lowered her menu and looked at him questioningly. "I thought you and Holly had plans for us already."

Great. Chalk up one more epic failure. The girlfriend who couldn't cook her way into a job at a fast food kitchen.

"We had some ideas," Adam started, pausing to clear his throat. "We thought we could do dinner at the manor. Maybe invite some of our local friends to join in the celebration."

Oh, thank the stars. Lacey and Evangeline could help me like they had on Thanksgiving. I offered Bella a confident smile. "Any special requests?"

"Mort likes pecan pudding and Adam's favorite is—" She stopped herself and gave a crafty smile. "Well of course, you already know Adam's favorite dish."

I glanced at Adam. "As far as I know, Adam loves all food equally."

Adam chuckled but Bella's lips didn't so much as twitch. "Actually it's pumpkin pie. But then, I suppose all we should really ask is for you to stay out of handcuffs for the duration of the celebration."

"Mom," Adam hissed.

Bella shrugged one shoulder. "It should go without saying, but as a precautionary bit of advice, I thought I would put it out there."

My cheeks flamed and I buried myself behind my menu, silently steaming. Adam draped an arm around my chair and I took some comfort in the small gesture of protection, but it couldn't take away the sting from the verbal slap his mother had just delivered. Who did she think she was? Just because she was the perfect shifter who married a shifter and lived by the haven rules without question, that made her better than everyone else?

"I think what your mother means, is that we'd like to have a calm, peaceful evening," Mort said after a long moment.

"No," Adam growled. "I don't think that's what she meant. We discussed this, Mother."

I peeked over my menu as Bella gave a long-suffering sigh. "My apologies."

"Not to me," Adam replied tersely. "To Holly."

Bella swiveled her eyes to me in slow motion and gave a slight nod. "I'm sorry, Holly. That was uncalled for."

I retreated back behind my menu. "It's fine, Bella."

Adam leaned in, his jaw tight. "This is my life. My girl-friend. My future. That's all you really need to know. If you guys don't want to be a part of it then you are more than welcome to go back home to your snooty little neighbor-hood and have Yule dinner with all your snobby friends."

Mort dropped his menu. "That's enough, Adam."

Adam scoffed. "I don't think so, Dad. I made myself crys-tal-clear on where I stand. Your snide comments and judg-ments aren't going to sway me, so save your breath."

I squirmed in my seat. This was getting stickier than Evangeline's old soap opera. "I think I'm going to go back to the manor," I said, pushing my menu aside.

Adam reached for my wrist. "Holly, no. You don't have to—"

I moved out of his reach and stood from the table. "It's fine. I'm getting a headache anyway." I grabbed my coat from the back of my chair and hurried to bundle back into its warmth. "I'll see you later."

Adam tried to protest, but didn't stop me as I left them and made a beeline for the front doors.

Outside, the air was crisp and clear and I decided to take the long way through town to get back home instead of going straight to the manor. I pocketed my hands and strolled down the street, fighting off the hot tears pushing against the backs of my eyes. At the end of the street, I stopped to let a lone car go by. I stared up at the stars, wishing they had the answers to my questions. If only they could untangle all of my dark worries and mixed emotions.

I considered calling one of my friends, but didn't want to interrupt their evenings. Cassie would tell me something cheery. She'd assure me that it wasn't as bad as it looked. Nick would clam up and tell me something practical, like to keep my chin up and it would all work out. Evangeline liked to talk about dating but I got the feeling that she had more experience with short-term relationships, so I'm not sure what her advice would be. And Lacey ... well Lacey was probably still angry at me for my behavior at Raven. As for Posy, she was still adjusting to the scandal of Adam and I dating while living under the same roof and likely wouldn't have anything helpful to offer, either.

It was times like this when I missed my mother the most. She'd always been a well of information for me and even if she didn't have any advice, she could stroke my hair and tell me that it was all going to be okay in the end. And I'd believe her. Tears blurred my vision, making the stars sparkle and shine as they melded together.

My cell phone rang and jerked me from my tangled thoughts. I fished in the deep pockets of my coat searching for the slim device and wondered who it was. Surely Adam was still at McNally's, probably trying to talk his parents into giving me a second—or was I on my third?—chance. Cassie would be with Chief Lincoln. Evangeline had seemed pretty cozy with Teddy.

I found the phone, tugged it free, and groaned at the display: Harvey Colepepper.

"Great," I grumbled, sliding my finger across the screen to answer the call. "Hello, Harvey."

"Holly, have you been able to get any more information?"

"Nice to hear from you too, Harvey," I quipped as I started across the street.

"This is business, Holly. I need to know what's going on. You're my eyes and ears, remember?"

"How could I forget?"

"Holly!"

"Fine, fine." I sighed. "Let's see, the woman with the victim was identified. Her name is Naomi Givens. As far as I know, the cops haven't found her yet. Oh, also, there's the minor detail that her husband confessed to the murder and the cops have him in custody."

For a moment I wished we were face to face so that I could see his eyes bug out after I dropped that bomb.

"What?" Harvey bellowed.

I pulled the phone away from my face. "Volume, Harvey. I don't think a new set of ear drums was included in our original agreement."

"What in the Otherworld happened?" he barked.

As I continued up the hill toward the manor, I found myself wishing for a massive mug of tea and my fuzzy slippers. I filled him in on the arrest as well as the information that I'd gleaned from Dread. By the time I reached the front porch, he was up to speed.

"It's obvious that this Gus person has been glamoured."

"Thanks for the tip, Harvey," I replied with a dash of sarcasm. "I'd already figured that. I just don't know *who* glamoured him. If Dread's information is correct, then we need to be looking at Greyson Molder himself and that seems ..."

"Out of your league?" Harvey said, throwing a bite of sarcasm back my way.

I clenched my teeth. "This entire thing is out of my league, Harvey! But that didn't stop you from shoving me into the deep end. I'm not an SPA agent or anything remotely close to it."

I didn't mention the part where my own life was rapidly

deteriorating and that I probably shouldn't be trusted to do much more than mope and wallow for at least the next twenty-four hours. Sure, eating your problems away might not be a good long-term strategy, but I was convinced that half a dozen Lemon Clouds would go quite a way toward solving my immediate problems.

"I need information, Holly. I don't have time to come back to town. Everything is going crazy here. Every SPA agent available is tracking down the various members of the Vampire Council and it's going to implode at any moment. Tempers are running high and I fully expect things to turn nasty. If we're not careful there will be a full-on uprising!"

An uprising of vampires? I shuddered at the thought. My academy history books detailed the events of the last vampire uprising and it hadn't been pretty.

I sighed heavily and squeezed my eyes closed. "What do you want me to do, Harvey? What do you need to know?"

"Go talk to the widow again. If she's really with Greyson Molder, she knows more than what she's told you. Use caution though, Holly. She's still mortal as far as we know."

"So I can't blast her with a stunning spell?"

"Holly …"

"Fine! I'll play nice."

"See that you do. And call me as soon as you're done."

"Aye, aye, captain."

"Is that supposed to be funny?"

I shrugged. "I thought so."

Harvey hung up and I sighed.

So much for the fuzzy slippers …

~

AS EXPECTED, Georgia was just about as thrilled when I showed up on her doorstop as I was to be there. She answered the door with a scowl. "What are you doing here?" she hissed. "I fired that quack of a PI you work with and he went and conned the cops out of my reward money!" She growled to herself. "It doesn't matter anymore. This whole nightmare is finally over. They caught the man who murdered my Paul. Now, leave me alone."

"See, that's the thing, Georgia, I don't think they did."

Her expression twisted. "What are you talking about?"

"The man who confessed to killing your husband is under a powerful spell."

Georgia scoffed and rolled her eyes. "Right. And my next door neighbor is the Easter Bunny."

"I'm serious, Georgia."

She narrowed her eyes at me as she cocked her hips and folded her arms. "Go away, little witch. I'm not interested in your crackpot theory. My husband's murderer is in jail. That's all that matters."

"Even if that's all a lie and you're sleeping next to the real murderer?"

Georgia's blue eyes went wide and her full lips parted.

"Let me inside and I'll explain."

She considered me for a moment and then, with a sigh, backed up and waved me inside. I hurried over the threshold and waited for her to close and lock the front door. As she reached for the lock, I noticed the Thraxis medallion was missing from around her neck.

"You have five minutes," she said, storming ahead of me back through the house to the kitchen. Apparently that was where she preferred to hold her meetings, although I wasn't sure why. It wasn't like she was offering me a cup of tea or a plate of cookies.

I squared off against her, the large granite island sepa-rating us. "I received some information that Paul and

Greyson were involved in some kind of business dealing. Is that true?"

"Who told you that?"

"It doesn't matter. Were they doing business together?"

Georgia thought for a moment and then shook her head. "No. They never met one another."

I considered her, wondering if she was the liar or if Dread was the one toying with me. "Have you ever met Dread? Greyson's second?"

Georgia nodded. "Once or twice. He takes care of Greyson's security."

"Uh huh. And what do you think about him?"

"Why?" Georgia snapped, her eyes narrowing again.

"Because he told me that Greyson is the one who killed Paul."

I waited, watching for her reaction, but she kept her stony mask firmly in place as she snorted. "That's ridiculous. Honestly, this is a waste of my time."

I gave her a pointed look. "Where's the necklace Greyson gave you? Trouble in undead paradise?"

Georgia snarled. "I don't see how that's any of your concern."

I sighed heavily. "Listen, Georgia, I don't want to fight with you. Just answer my questions and I'll leave. I don't know what Greyson has told you about the supernatural world, but there are probably a lot of things he left out. That medallion is more than just some pretty necklace he wanted you to have as a gift. It's a dangerous talisman that was enchanted by a powerful witch."

Georgia's hand floated to the place where the necklace should have been hanging. Her fingers grasped the air and she quickly dropped her hand. "It was giving me a rash, so I took it off."

"A rash?" Something clicked in the back of my mind and I took a pace backwards. "Georgia, did Greyson—"

"Turn me?" she asked, smiling for the first time since she'd answered the door. Two fangs glistened as her smile widened and a chill ran down my spine. "Why, yes. Yes he did."

CHAPTER 20

"*S*ee, little witch, I don't have to be afraid of you anymore. Greyson warned me to stay away from other supernaturals. Said they won't give me the same level of *nutrition* as humans, but in this case, I'd wager that he'd let me make an exception." Georgia's silky voice was laced with an icy chill as she slowly rounded the kitchen island.

I forced myself to stay rooted in place. The last thing I needed was for her to think I was afraid of her. Even though I would have been a fool not to be. Newly turned vampires were especially powerful, and apparently Georgia had missed the lesson about not eating live ...

Georgia reclined back against the island, her fingers sliding over the smooth stone as she surveyed me. "You might not know this, but Greyson is an incredibly private individual. He wouldn't like you showing up here at night with a bunch of questions."

"So it doesn't bother you that your new lover killed your husband? That doesn't even concern you?"

Georgia frowned. "Greyson didn't kill Paul. And they didn't have business dealings together. Dread is lying."

"Why would he do that? Greyson is his ... lord ... or whatever you vampires would call it."

"I don't know *why*. All I know is that he is. I'll see to it that Greyson deals with him. The police chief already came and told me the news. Paul was killed because he was sleeping with the wrong woman. Her husband killed him. I've never even met the man before."

"And you don't think that maybe he was glamoured into confessing? It doesn't strike you as odd that someone would give such a full confession out of the blue like that?"

Georgie shrugged. "People crack. He probably had a guilty conscious."

"But what if Greyson is lying to you, Georgia?"

She slammed her hands on the counter, sending a loud boom through the expansive kitchen. "Stop it! Greyson didn't do this. He wouldn't have! We tell each other every-thing." She stalked toward me, one finger pointed in my face. "He has no reason to lie to me."

Oh, of course not. A bloodthirsty vampire was probably a highly reliable boyfriend. Was she for real?

"Did Greyson tell you that the Thraxis medallion causes a disease to vampires that wear it?" I asked, stalling for time. Magic buzzed at my fingertips but I had to wait for the right moment. Stunning Georgia would only give me a few seconds to get away.

She stopped in her tracks. "A disease?"

"Yes. When the necklace was made, the Molder family trapped a witch and forced her to enchant it. See, they wanted something that would allow the wearer to go into daylight without the unfortunate side effects." I paused and cocked my head. "He *did* tell you that part, right?"

Georgia's nostrils flared. "Of *course*."

I shrugged casually. "Just checking."

"Get to the point, witch."

I sighed. "The witch cursed the necklace and now any vampire that wears it will be stricken with a fatal disease."

Georgia crossed her arms. "Well Greyson gave it to me when I was still a mortal. Maybe he didn't know about the disease."

I snorted. "You really believe that?"

"Enough! The necklace doesn't matter. Greyson didn't kill Paul and I'm done with your questions. Get out of my house before I turn you into an appetizer!" She bared her fangs, this time with a menacing growl. "Do your little magic trick and disappear."

I held up my hands, not bothering to hide the glowing magic pooled in each palm. "I'll go, but I'm warning you, Georgia. Greyson is not some Prince Charming. He's a power-hungry murderer that's conspiring with a ring of other powerful houses to overthrow the Supernatural Protection Agency and the Haven Council. I won't bore you with the details, but I was caught in a strikingly similar situation once upon a time. Granted I had a better tan and—ya know—my soul. I get it. All right? I get the allure of power and charisma. But this is going to be a war, Georgia, and I can guarantee you don't want to be caught in the middle of it."

Without waiting, I reached for the Larkspur and within a blink of an eye, found myself in the dimly lit parking lot in front of the old liquor store. I hurried around to the back and knocked on the door, silently pleading with whoever would listen that the password hadn't changed since my last visit.

The glowing outline of the door appeared and gruff voice said, "Password?"

"Gingersnap?"

The door opened and I was ushered forward by a different guard; this one less intimidating that the last one.

The club was decorated in a Moroccan blue with gold accents, and some kind of exotic music was playing. "What in the Otherworld? Some kind of 'round the world' theme going on here?" It was like Taco Tuesday, but for decor.

Dread wasn't hard to find. He was holding down the same table as last time. He didn't even seem that surprised to see me back in the club again as I approached his table. "Well, well, well," he purred. "I was wondering when you'd be back to see your old friend Dread."

"We are *not* friends," I said, sliding into the opposite booth.

His smile stayed firmly in place. "What can I do for you, witchling?"

I glanced around the club, wondering if I'd made the right decision by coming. I needed to get answers for Harvey. And for myself. But Dread wasn't exactly a reliable source. Or if he was, it would be nearly impossible to prove. At the moment, it was his word against Georgia's and both of their stories were radically different than the confession of the self-proclaimed killer.

"Come on. Spit it out. I don't have all night, darling." Dread said, interrupting my thoughts. "Well, actually I do. But that's not the point." He laughed at his own joke. "What do you want?"

I sighed and splayed my hands over the table top. "I just paid a little visit to Georgia Banks. She insists that her husband and Greyson weren't in business together. And if they weren't in the middle of some kind of business dispute as you claim, then I'm left wondering if the rest of your story is true."

"Of course that's what she said. She didn't know about their business deal."

"I don't understand."

Dread sighed like I was trying his patience. He leaned

forward on the table, all pretense of charm gone. "Listen, witch, this goes beyond some small-town murder investigation, all right? There are things at play here that would make your pretty little head spin. I don't know why you're even trying to get involved."

The tips of my fingers tingled as magic percolated to life. He was one snide comment away from getting blasted up to the rafters. "You and your kind might not care about this case, but a man lost his life and now an innocent man is going to take the fall for it. I can't let that happen."

Dread laughed and shook his head. "One of those justice junkies, huh?"

"I've been called worse."

"All right, I'll make you a deal then. You want to take Greyson down, then I'll help you. But you have to bring me the Thraxis medallion."

I leveled him with an unflinching stare. "Why would you do that? You're his second in command. If you turn on him, the rest of the Molders will eat you for breakfast."

Dread gave a Cheshire grin. "You still don't get it, do you, little witch?"

"Tell me what I'm missing then." I crossed my arms tightly over my chest and glared at him. "Please enlighten me to your evil genius."

Dread laughed and kicked back in his chair as casually as if he were watching a football game with a big bowl of potato chips in his lap. "The Molders won't know it was me who turned him in. As his second, I'll automatically assume power."

"You sure they won't know?" I glanced around the club. No one was paying much attention to us, but that didn't mean there weren't a few ears cocked in our direction. "You're not exactly trying to keep this under wraps."

Dread hitched a shoulder. "These are my people. This

whole club is full of vamps who'd rather see me in power. Greyson is ignoring the true needs of his people because he's too busy playing politics."

"And that's why you want the medallion."

"Bingo. Maybe there's some hope for you yet, little witchling."

"What makes you think the medallion's powers will work for you?"

Dread considered me for a long moment, as though debating how much he could say. "Let's just say that I've spent a very long time learning everything about that medallion and the curse that it carries. I'm confident I can break the spell and unlock its powers. After that, I'll be king of the vampires. So it doesn't really matter to me whether you get Greyson out of my way or I have to do it myself. I'll find a way with or without your assistance. If you're smart, you'll accept my offer and get what you want out of the deal."

I pushed away from the table. "I'll think about it."

"Think quickly. Otherwise it will be too late for your little human friend, Gus."

I didn't bother correcting him that Gus and I weren't friends. We'd never even met before. "And why is that?"

"Because once he goes to trial and confesses, it will be a whole lot harder for him to wriggle out of his sentence. I'm not in the jailbreaking business."

I was borderline impressed with his knowledge of the human court system and slightly annoyed at myself for having had to ask. "Fine. I'll come back tomorrow night. Will you be here?"

"Waiting on pins and needles," he replied with a smarmy grin.

Without bothering with niceties, I left the club and used the Larkspur to get me back to the manor. As soon as my feet hit the manor property line, I bolted for the privacy of my greenhouse and whipped out my phone. Each ring spanned on forever but Harvey finally answered and I launched into my request without pausing for breath. "I don't have time to explain, but Harvey, do you still have the replica of the Thraxis medallion that your crafter made?"

"Yes. Why?"

I paced to the other side of the greenhouse and peered through the tinted windows to keep watch on the backyard. I had the distinct feeling that I'd somehow been followed or was being watched, even though I'd used the Larkspur to get home and would have been virtually untraceable to a vampire. But what if Dread had sent someone to my house? He knew Lacey and I were roommates. Maybe he knew where she lived. I squeezed my eyes closed and tried to push back the panicked thoughts and theories swelling inside me. "I need it."

"Holly, that replica was only for identification purposes. It doesn't have any power and won't hold up under magical scrutiny."

"I know that." I paced back to the other side of the green-house and wished that I'd gone inside and retrieved Boots. He would have calmed me. He wasn't exactly built to be a security guard, but his presence would have made me feel less jumpy. The yard looked still and quiet. The only things moving were the tall grass and tree branches that were swaying in the gentle coastal breeze. "I have a plan, Harvey. But for it to work, I need the medallion."

Harvey sighed impatiently. "Holly, I didn't bring you into this case to go off on half-cocked theories with some mysterious plan. If you have information, then you need to come into my office. We will come up with something together. I can unlock the portal for you if you want to come in."

I nodded. "Okay, fine. But it has to be tomorrow morning and I need to leave your office with that replica."

"We'll talk," Harvey replied coolly.

I bit back a growl of frustration. "Fine!"

"Ten o'clock. Use the portal I showed you. You do remember where it is located, don't you?"

"Yes," I bit out through gritted teeth.

"Very good. Until then."

Harvey clicked off the call and I resisted the urge to smash the phone with a gardening trowel. Why didn't he trust me? After all, without my information, he'd still be in Beechwood Harbor looking for leads. In a matter of days I'd managed to find a connection to the Vampire Council. Without me, the SPA would continue hacking at the hydra without making any progress. You'd think he'd at least be a little more encouraging.

I sighed and scanned the tree line one more time before turning back to the door of the greenhouse. Movement caught my eye and I froze in place. "Who's there? Show yourself!"

A form moved in the shadows and before I could conjure a stunning spell, a thin voice begged, "Please, don't hurt me."

I shifted the magic in my hand and threw a ball of blue light into the space between me and the silhouette. The light revealed a thin, cloaked woman. "Who are you?"

The woman reached up with trembling hands and lowered her hood. She had long, tangled brunette hair and a pretty, though slightly gaunt, face. I tilted my head, trying to figure out where I'd seen her before, when it hit me. I gasped.

CHAPTER 21

"*N*aomi? What are you doing here?" I asked when I found my voice.

Naomi glanced around nervously. "Can you dim that light?" she asked softly. "I can't be seen here."

I considered her request for a moment. She looked like she hadn't eaten or slept in days. Probably not since the murder. I could easily take her on myself. But there was a part of me that was hesitant to turn out the light. What if it was some kind of trick? After all, Dread had told me she was one of them. "Are you a vampire?" I asked her.

"No!" Her eyes went wide. "Why would you even say something like that?"

"Okay. Okay." I held up a hand and lowered the light. It was just faint enough that I could still make out her face but that anyone looking inside wouldn't be able to see us. "I'm sorry. I was given bad information ..."

A flicker of fire lit behind her dark eyes. "Let me guess, Dread told you I was one of *them*."

I sighed. "Yes."

The adrenaline drained from my system and I suddenly wanted to crawl into bed and sleep for three days. Between the murder investigation, SPA drama, and Adam's parents, I was ready to crash and burn.

"I'm not a vampire," Naomi said firmly. She looked out the window again and licked her lips.

"He said you work with them. Is that part true?"

She returned her worried gaze to mine and after a moment, gave a tiny nod. "Regrettably."

"I don't understand."

"It's a long story." She twisted her fingers in her cloak and tugged nervously at the fabric. "I got tangled up with the wrong crowd a few years ago and ended up owing a debt I couldn't possibly pay. Not without my husband finding out. I met a man, Greyson, and he made me a deal. In exchange for the debt to be covered, I would work for the vampires. Obviously with their limitations there are certain things they can't do. So I do them on their behalf. At first it was simple things, like going to meetings that had to be held during daylight hours, and taking care of real estate showings for their expanding businesses. But then the demands got … darker. They forced me into scouting certain types of people."

"So you were looking for humans they could turn?" I asked. The idea alone was enough to turn my stomach.

Naomi dropped her chin in a solemn nod. "I'm not proud of it."

"Wait—were you the one who found Georgia Banks?"

She nodded again. "That's right. I met her at an open house and after two complimentary mimosas, she was spilling her guts to me. She told me all about her miserable marriage and how she was trying to get out of her pre-nup so she could get her husband's money. She was the perfect target: rich, naive, and very pretty. Greyson likes blondes."

"So what was the plan? You introduce her to Greyson and he offers to turn her, and in exchange, he got her husband out of the way?"

"What?" Naomi's eyes snapped open wide. "No. No! Greyson didn't kill Paul Banks."

"He didn't?"

Naomi shook her head. "No. Greyson wanted Georgia and Paul alive!"

"Okay, back up. I'm confused. I thought Greyson was turning these people so they could join his House. He's building an army."

"He wanted Paul and Georgia's money and connections. Paul Banks was an investment banker and his firm has some of the state's most successful businesses on their client list. Greyson isn't looking to build an army of vampires. He's trying to rise up against the haven system. Once it's broken, he plans to come out of the coffin. In a very big way."

My mouth dropped open. "You don't mean ..."

Naomi nodded. "Unfortunately, I do."

If Greyson Molder overthrew the haven system and put his Vampire Council into place, there would be no one to stop vampires from taking over, especially if they actually managed to unlock the Thraxis medallion and were able to go into daylight. They would be unstoppable. The entire SPA wouldn't be able to contain them. It would be an all-out war and the humans would be the ones to pay the price.

"Bats! This is so much worse than I ever imagined." I paced back and forth a few times, my mind swimming with images from my academy textbooks that depicted the last vampire uprising. "Okay. Let me slow down. Obviously something went wrong with his plan. If he didn't plan on being with Georgia, then why did he agree to turn her?"

"She was looking for an escape. I lured her to Raven one night. It was all a set up. She met Greyson and that was kind of it …" Naomi swallowed hard. "Turning her into a vampire was the one thing he could promise her to string her along. He filled her head with all sorts of gothic romance and she fell for it."

I folded my arms. "Well I just saw her about an hour ago and I can assure you that she is all vamp now."

Naomi cursed under her breath, though she didn't seem too surprised by the revelation.

"And what about Paul? You were there. What did you see? If it wasn't Greyson that killed him, then who was it?"

"Dread was there."

A shudder coursed through me at the whispered name.

Naomi shoved her hair back. "See, Greyson was the one who made the bargain with me. I was bound to the Molder family, to do their bidding until my debt was paid. At first, I only reported to Greyson. But as he got deeper and deeper into his plans and schemes, he turned me over to Dread, who lived to torment me." She paused and dragged in a slow breath. I could only imagine the things he'd put her through. "I got desperate. Really desperate. I did some things I wasn't proud of to make some money. I thought if I could pay back my debt, I could get away." She gave a hollow laugh and chewed on her lower lip. "I was so stupid."

"No. You weren't." Pity surged up inside my chest. The woman standing before me might have made some bad decisions, but she certainly didn't deserve the things that had happened since. And now she was putting her very life on the line to try to make it right. "You did what you had to do to survive, Naomi. You can't cross vampires like Greyson and Dread and live to tell about it."

She sniffled. "A lot of good it did. Now my husband will pay the ultimate price. And everything I did was to protect him!"

"Who glamoured him? Was it Dread?"

She nodded. "He came to the house two nights ago. I was in the kitchen making dinner, and Gus invited him in. He didn't know …," her voice trailed off and she dissolved into tears. "I came out and there they were, sitting on the couch together. It was too late. Gus' eyes were glazed over like some kind of puppet, and he was repeating everything Dread told him. By the time I dis-invited him, it was too late. Gus kept babbling over and over again that he'd killed Paul. He wept. Begged for my forgiveness and then … then he got angry. So angry. I'd never seen him like that before. He called me all kinds of names and screamed at me to get out of the house."

"Where have you been since then?" I asked softly. "Do you have someplace safe to stay?"

She nodded. "I've been with a friend that Dread doesn't know about. But I had to come see you. I was hoping you could help."

"How did you even find me?"

"I was at Raven the night you and your friend came in. I saw you talking to Dread and then you stormed out. Everyone was talking about it. No one talks to Dread like that and gets away with it. I followed your friend back here that night, but I didn't know what to say to you. So I left after a few minutes. But then after Gus got arrested, I decided I couldn't wait anymore. I needed to tell someone the truth."

"I'm glad you came, but to be honest, I'm not sure how much help I can be."

Naomi clutched my arm desperately. "Please, you have to help my husband. He can't go to prison for something he didn't do. He shouldn't have to suffer for my mistakes."

My stomach twisted into a knot at the pain and desperation in her eyes. "I want to help, Naomi. Really, I do."

I wanted to tell her about my current plan and assure her it would all work flawlessly and that her husband would go free and she would be rid of the threat hanging over her head. But I couldn't. The plan was still piecing together in my mind and I wasn't sure that Harvey would be willing to go along with it. He might dismiss me and tell me they would handle it. Which, based on my past interactions with the SPA, I didn't have a lot of faith in.

But I certainly wasn't going to tell Naomi that.

"Can you tell me what you saw that night? When Paul was murdered? I work with a PI and if we can come up with some solid proof that Gus wasn't anywhere near that hotel, maybe we can get him out of jail."

Naomi nodded and dried the tears from her face. "Paul and I had gone on a *date* before. At that same hotel. He called me. I remember thinking it was a little early, but he was really upset and said he didn't want to be alone. He needed to blow off some steam. I met him at the bar up the road."

"The Grasshopper?"

She nodded. "We had a drink, talked, flirted. It was nice. I liked Paul. He was always kind to me. Anyway, we left and went to the hotel and up to the room. But before anything happened, the window broke and Dread swooped inside. He was angry at me for working off the books. He hit Paul and when I screamed, he choked me. He attacked Paul and I ran. I thought he was dead. There was so much blood."

"Did you go out into the hallway?"

"No. They were in front of the door so I went out the window. There was a balcony. I jumped off. I didn't know what else to do. I was so scared."

"That was two stories up!"

"I know. It was stupid." She shook her head like she still couldn't quite believe it. "I jumped and landed in some bushes off to the side. As soon as I hit the ground I just started running. I got to the bar and hopped in my car and just started driving. I didn't stop until three in the morning when I ran out of gas. I was almost to the border and decided to stop at a hotel for the night."

"I'm so sorry, Naomi. That sounds awful."

She shuddered. "It was terrifying. I keep dreaming it over and over again. It's like I can't escape from the memories or stop thinking about that poor man. If I hadn't been with him that night, he'd still be alive."

"You can't blame yourself, Naomi." I moved away from the window and the orb of light bounced behind me as I stooped to retrieve a woven basket from a shelf. I'd stashed some of my potions there when Harvey had first shown up at the manor. I searched through the pile until I found one labeled Sweet Dreams. I turned to Naomi and handed her the vial. "Here, try this. It will give you dreamless sleep. Just one drop in your nightly cup of tea should do it."

She took the vial from me and inspected it. "Really?"

I nodded.

"Thank you so much." She moved for the door.

"Naomi?"

She stopped and looked at me over her shoulder.

"Do you think you could get Greyson to Raven tomorrow night? I have a plan. I'm still working out the details, but I think I have a way to make this all right."

Naomi nodded slowly. "I know I can."

"Dread told me that Raven is full of his people. Is that true?"

"Yes and no. These days it's mostly Dread's playhouse. But if Greyson decides to show up, I can guarantee his lackeys will be right behind him."

"The Vampire Council members?"

"Yes."

A bubble of panic swelled in the pit of my stomach. The plan was coming together, but as each new step built on the last, a dozen new scenarios of how it could all go wrong started to creep in. It had to work or else everything would fall apart. And not just in Beechwood Harbor.

CHAPTER 22

I called in a favor and had Paisley pick up my shift. In theory, the idea was to come up with a plan, but I ended up spending the entire morning pacing, tangled in my own thoughts. Eventually, Posy told me that I was wearing trenches in the hard wood floors and suggested I needed a cup of tea. While I was in the kitchen waiting for the water to heat, Lacey came down from her room and pushed into the kitchen.

"I didn't know you were in here," she said, pausing at the door like she wasn't sure if she should stay or go.

I sighed. "Lacey, come on, you can't still be mad at me."

She frowned. "Oh, believe me, I *can*."

I scoffed and finished making my tea. "Fine. Stay mad. I've got enough on my plate without figuring out how to appease you."

Lacey stalked to the fridge. "Good! Because I'm not in a forgiving mood."

"Shocking," I muttered to myself as I took my cup to the table.

A tense silence filled the room, making it feel stuffy

despite the somewhat chilly temperature. Lacey dawdled at the counter, pouring her lunch into a crystal goblet. After a few minutes, I heaved a sigh. "Okay, fine. I'm sorry, Lacey. I wasn't trying to make a scene at Raven. And I never thanked you for helping me."

"You're welcome," Lacey sniffed. "After all, I'm not the one deluding myself that I can be some kind of super spy."

"That's what you think I'm doing? Playing games?"

She shrugged and took a long sip.

"For your information, I'm going to Harvey's office in an hour to tell him exactly how to bust this whole Vampire Council. Oh, and by the way, your buddy Dread, he's a cold-blooded killer!"

Lacey slowly set her goblet down. "What do you mean? *He's* the one who killed that man?"

I nodded. "That's right."

"But—wait, why would he—he couldn't have been the one."

"It was him, Lacey. And he's trying to frame Greyson so that he can take over the entire Molder House."

She straightened. "We have to do something!"

I sighed. "Did you miss the part about me going to see Harvey?"

"We have to go now!"

"Relax, princess. I have an appointment and nothing is going to happen until tonight anyway. In case you haven't noticed, the sun's still out."

She sagged back against the counter but her expression was tight and her eyes continued to dart back and forth as the puzzle pieces fell into place for her. "I can't believe that little rat! Do you know he tried to hit on me?"

I rolled my eyes. "Yes, clearly *that's* the most disturbing thing going on here now. Some lowlife tried to sweet talk you." I stood from the table and swept my mug up. "Honestly, Lacey …"

I shoved through the swinging kitchen door and headed toward my bedroom. As I passed the front door, a loud knock startled me and a stream of hot tea sloshed over the edge of my overfull mug and burnt my hand. "Bats!" I cursed. "Who on earth could that be?"

I checked the peephole and saw Harvey standing on the front porch. I hurried to open the door and he marched inside. "Change of plans," he declared, crossing over the welcome mat.

"What are you doing here?"

He stopped in the center of the foyer and spun around. "Close the door, Holly. We can't risk being overheard. Who's here right now?"

I looked around, mentally counting off my roommates. Evangeline would be at The Emerald, working. Posy was probably in the attic or maybe out with Gwen. And Adam had promised to take his parents out for the day after the disastrous dinner the night before. "Lacey is the only one home and she already knows what's going on." Harvey scowled up at me. "Just deal with it. I needed her help."

"Fine. Where can we talk?"

I led the way into the study and closed the door behind us. Harvey heaved himself into one of the two tall, wingback chairs in front of the fireplace and I sent a blast of fire into the hearth as I took my own seat. "Is there a problem at the office? I was about to leave to come see you."

Harvey shifted, his legs dangling off the chair, and pulled a small box from his pocket. "I can't trust that we won't be overheard. We discovered that there are some Vampire Council supporters in the SPA ranks."

"Great."

Harvey glared at me before holding out the box. "Here is

the replica." I reached for it but he tugged it out of my reach. "First, you tell me what your plan is."

I hurried to explain everything I'd learned—the tidbits of information about the medallion, the true murderer, and the glamoured human who was lined up to take the fall. As I went on, Harvey's expression became darker and deep worry lines etched his face.

"This is much worse than I expected," he said when I was done. "We have to act tonight."

"I agree. Naomi isn't safe as long as Dread is still free, and her husband is days away from going to prison for a crime he didn't commit. Not to mention the whole vamps-taking-over-the-world thing."

Harvey gave a sage nod. "What's your plan?"

I took a deep breath, hoping that what I was about to explain didn't sound completely insane.

~

AT HALF PAST MIDNIGHT, I arrived at Raven's back door, alone and dressed head to toe in black. My heart was slamming inside my chest like a jackrabbit and the pounding in my head made it hard to think. There were about three dozen things that could go wrong in the next few hours, most of which would result in my own deaths. Harvey hadn't been thrilled with my plan, but in the end he'd had no other options and had reluctantly agreed to it.

Naomi had called two hours before and told me that Greyson had rounded up his followers and was planning to be at the club at midnight. I'd given them a little time to get comfortable and—if I was lucky—a little tipsy. But I couldn't stall any longer. It was time to make my move.

I raised my hand and knocked on the back door. The mysterious, disembodied voice asked me for the password and I rattled off the one Naomi had given me. The small doorway appeared and opened for me. A large guard appeared from the shadows and gave me a once-over. "You again?"

I recognized him as the one from my first visit. "What can I say? I like the ambiance."

He grunted and let me pass. I strode into the club but felt his eyes following me as I went. I briefly wondered if the security had been warned to be extra alert since the Molder heir was present. I ignored the guard's attention and moved farther into the club, scanning the outskirts of the room and the occupants of each table as casually as possible. I could almost see Dread's normal table, but before I could get a good look, a group of vampires passed in front of me without so much as an apology as they jostled me.

"Excuse you," I grumbled, squeezing between two of them.

A hand reached for me and tugged me back before I could get past and magic pulsed on my hand, ready to fire. I whipped around to confront the two vamps, but instead found myself staring into Georgia Banks' eyes. Only, instead of the sharp, fiery eyes I was used to, they were dull grey and sunken far into their sockets.

"Georgia?" My mouth dropped open. Inflamed lines wound around her neck in a spiderweb pattern. I couldn't help but stare and Georgia—for once—didn't look perturbed by my presence. "Georgia, are you okay? What happened to you?"

"The necklace," she croaked, her voice scratchy and nearly inaudible over the pulsing music piped throughout the club. She reached up and gingerly traced the red marks in her translucent skin. Her golden tan was gone and it looked like she'd lost an alarming amount of weight overnight. "You were right."

"The necklace did this to you?"

She nodded. "It was a rash ... now this ..." She licked her lips and I had the urge to go get her a tall glass of ice water, though it wouldn't physically do her any good.

"What are you doing here?" I asked, shuffling out of the way as another cluster of vampires came through. I cast a glance around the room. There were nearly twice as many people as the last time I'd been there. It could only mean that Greyson was here and that Naomi had held up her end of the bargain. I needed to get to him in order to follow through with the plan. I didn't have time for Georgia, but at the same time, I couldn't leave her.

The old flare returned to Georgia's eyes. "I'm here to see him."

I craned around to see where she was looking. Dread's table was now within sight; the cluster of vampires had moved on. A tall, broad-shouldered vampire sat beside Dread and the two were laughing together like they'd just shared some kind of inside joke. A blonde walked by, hips swinging, and they both stared after her.

Georgia still had a grip on my arm and her nails dug into my skin as she watched Greyson's eyes stray. "Ouch!" I yelped. She released me, but didn't offer an apology. I tugged my arm back and rubbed the spot where her nails had broken the skin. "Listen, Georgia, you should leave. Confronting him here, with all his people around—it's not going to end well."

Her eyes snapped back to mine. "I'm dying, Holly. He killed me. This time for good."

"What are you going to do?" I asked, already knowing I didn't like the answer.

She narrowed her eyes, locking them onto Greyson as though they could shoot lasers and turn him to dust from across the room. "I'm going to take him with me."

Bats.

Without waiting, Georgia stalked across the room, heading straight for Greyson. I scrambled to follow her. My plan was about to be blown out of the water. I reached for her arm but fell short.

Greyson looked up and saw Georgia barreling toward him. His cool grey eyes registered panic for a moment but with a snap of his fingers, another vampire, this one twice his size, stepped between him and the blonde. "Stop right there," the guard warned Georgia.

"Get out of my way," she hissed.

The guard bared his fangs. Georgia did the same.

I backed up a step.

Greyson laughed and the sound echoed around the club as the other patrons fell silent. "Now, now, Georgia, what's this all about? You're not going to attack me in my own club, are you?"

"You did this to me," she growled savagely as she pointed to the marks on her neck. "I'm dying. Your *friends* need to know that this is what you do!"

Greyson looked unconcerned as his former lover stood brazenly before him, accusing him of the hideous act. "Go home, Georgia. This isn't a fight you want to pick."

She balled her hands and dug them into her hips. "I'm not leaving."

Greyson stared at her for a long moment and then jerked his chin at the guard. The guard stepped forward and reached for Georgia, but she was much smaller and quickly dodged out of his reach. In the blink of an eye, she was past the guard and at Greyson's throat. Beside him, Dread cast a glance around and then sat back in his seat.

"Tell them," Georgia demanded. "Tell them what you did to me! To my husband!"

Two vampires grabbed for Georgia and snagged her by

187

the arms. They tugged her away from their leader and she slumped down, defeated or simply too tired and weak to continue.

"Your husband?"

Dread shifted in his seat. "Get out of here, Georgia."

Georgia looked up at Greyson, her eyes full of tears. "My husband," she sobbed. "You killed him, for no—no good—reason!" The two vampires started to drag her away. "Just tell me why!"

Greyson frowned at her, maybe feeling a shred of pity. "Georgia, I'll admit to giving you the medallion to wear. Not to kill you, but to test and see if the curse had been broken."

My eyes snapped to Dread and watched his eyes go wide. "You gave it to *her*?" he hissed.

Greyson glared at his second, clearly perturbed by his blatant questioning. "What I do with *my* House heirloom is none of your concern."

A murmur swept through the room and as I looked around, I noticed more than a few sets of eyebrows were raised.

Greyson raised a hand. "I don't know anything about what happened to your husband, Georgia. Why would I? I already had what I wanted."

Georgia looked around wildly. "Then who did it? Who killed my Paul?"

"He did!" A voice pierced the crowd and I cringed.

I spun around and saw Naomi just as she threw off her cloak. Her arm was outstretched, finger pointing squarely at Dread. "He killed Paul Banks. I was there."

Greyson twisted in his seat, his eyes blazing as they landed on his second. "Is that true?"

Dread shrank back.

Georgia stared wide-eyed at the two vampires. "Why, Dread? What did Paul ever do to you?"

Dread narrowed his eyes in Naomi's direction. "He got in my way."

Naomi stalked forward. "I was never *yours*," she declared. "I was only with him to get away from you!"

Greyson glanced to a couple of vampires on the other side of the room and they surged forward to grab Dread. As he was being dragged out of the booth, he kicked and hissed. "Why does it matter what human I killed? Greyson's been doing it for years! Decades!"

"That's enough!" Greyson bellowed, shooting to his feet. "What I do, I do to keep the family alive. Not out of some petty jealousy!"

A booming voice followed a tremendous crash as beams of light bounced around the room. "SPA! Everyone get on the floor. Now!"

CHAPTER 23

ootsteps, screams, and angry shouts all melded together into a deafening roar. I spun around, unsure where to go or what to do. I scanned the crowd as it dissolved into chaos, looking for my SPA contact—a vampire that Harvey trusted—but with everyone running and tripping over those who had immediately followed the order to get on the ground, it was impossible. SPA agents in black jackets emblazoned with the bold white logo burst into every entry point and swarmed the crowd. Greyson, Dread, and the vampires with their hands on Georgia were all taken down by agents.

Georgia got on the ground, only to be hauled up moments later and taken out with a few other women from the crowd. A path opened and I moved for it. Prior to going into Raven, I'd met with the SPA agents on the task force, so they all let me pass without question as they rounded up the rest of the club-goers.

I pushed out of the exit and took a deep breath of the crisp evening air.

"Well that didn't exactly go as planned," a familiar voice said wryly.

I whirled around and found Harvey staring up at me. He was dressed in his official SPA gear and consulting the watch on his wrist. "I'm sorry."

He looked up at me and shrugged. "Doesn't matter to me how we get the bad guys, Holly. All that matters is that we get them. And an entire room full of witnesses just heard both the murder confession and the truth about what Greyson and his lackeys have been up to. It's a slam-dunk case."

"What will happen next?" I asked, nervously glancing over my shoulder as agents started filing out and loading their captives into the waiting bus.

"We will question everyone present and get the full narrative. The innocent will be released. The rest will be taken into custody until a trial can be held. Pretty standard."

"What about Georgia Banks?" I asked, still haunted by the marks around her neck.

Harvey nodded and I turned to follow his eyes. Georgia was being ushered out by an agent and shown to a car instead of the bus. "She'll be taken through the nearest portal and admitted to the Seattle haven hospital. I'm not sure what kind of curse was placed on the medallion, but the doctors there will be able to help her."

I swallowed hard, hoping he was right. She'd been through enough.

"And Naomi?"

"She'll be placed in protective custody until the trial is over. Then she will be free to go. In exchange for her testimony of course."

I wrapped my arms around myself. "And Gus?"

Harvey sighed. "That one is trickier. We will try to arrange for an intervention before his trial. He will be dosed with a potion that reverses the glamour effect, then the SPA will work to remove him from the human legal system and find a way to extract him from prison. Once that happens, he will be placed into protective custody, likely with his wife."

I wanted to ask more questions, but a fight broke out across the lot and Harvey raced forward to break it up. Two vampires waiting to be loaded onto the bus started fighting, ramming into one another and scratching with their cuffed hands. Harvey and two other agents ran forward to subdue them.

"Witch!" I spun around at the sharp voice and saw the refrigerator-sized doorman bolting for me, fire in his eyes. "This is all your doing! I can't prove it, but you brought this down on us! Filthy witch scum!" He lunged for me but I conjured a stunning spell so powerful that it knocked him backward as easily as if I was swatting a fly on a lazy summer afternoon.

I smirked as he hit the pavement. "For a big guy, that was way too easy. You should work on that," I said before stepping over him.

Through the curses of the vampire on the ground and the noise from the situation behind me, a voice cut through crystal-clear: "Holly?"

My heart jumped to my throat. Nick? No, it couldn't be.

I turned around and spotted him racing across the street. My pulse slammed in my ears, drowning out everything else. "What are you doing here?"

His face was ashen as he stared at the man on the ground. He'd seen the whole thing.

"Nick, I can explain—"

His eyes dropped to the man on the ground. "Did you just *kill* him?"

"No," I yelped, shaking my head frantically. "No. It was just a stunning spell."

"Spell?"

I squeezed my eyes closed.

"Holly, what is going on here? Why is your hand *glowing*?"

I glanced down at my hand, not having realized that another spell was right at my fingertips. I clenched my fist and forced myself to meet Nick's frantic eyes. There was no way I was going to be able to talk my way out of this one, so I opted for the truth. "I'm a witch, Nick."

"A *what*?"

"A witch."

Nick burst out laughing—the delirious, three-o'clock-in-the-morning-sugar-high kind of laugh.

"Harvey," I hissed, snagging him by the arm as he crossed in front of us.

Nick started to babble questions: "What can you do? Can you fly? Do you use a broomstick or is that some kind of witchy old wives' tale? Wait! Where's your wand?"

On and on and on.

Harvey tugged out of my grip and straightened his official SPA jacket. "What is it? We're a little busy here as you might have noticed."

I glanced at Nick and licked my lips. "He's … I had to tell him … about me. He saw me cast a stunning spell."

Nick looked from me to Harvey and then back again. He held up his hands. "Wait! Wait one second. You're not going to wipe my memory like they do in the movies are you?"

I winced. "I'm sorry, Nick. It has to be done."

"No, no. It doesn't. Please, Holly! You know I won't say anything!"

Harvey used his fingers to let out a loud whistle and then snapped his fingers in the direction of a tall man wielding a brass-handled wand. "Sinclair, we need a wipe."

Nick turned to me, his eyes full and pleading. "Holly,

please, don't let them do this. I don't want to forget everything that happened tonight."

"I'm sorry, Nick. We don't have a choice. It's policy."

His eyes went wide as the tall wizard approached. I held onto his arm and sucked in a deep breath to combat the tears pricking at my eyes. The panicked look on Nick's face made me want to beg for an exception, but I knew my pleas would fall on deaf ears. In this situation, there was no wiggle room in the SPA policies. Any human who had contact with the supernatural world had to be wiped. Period.

"It will be okay," I whispered, clinging tightly to his arm.

"Close your eyes," the wizard instructed as he raised his wand. He pointed it between Nick's eyes and waited until Nick followed his command. His blue eyes fluttered closed and small, pinched lines formed at the edges as he waited. "Very good. Hold still and we'll be done in just a flash."

The wizard whispered some ancient incantation—the words of which I recognized but didn't fully understand. Mind magic was extremely advanced and not something the Council let just anyone tinker with. Only those with a proclivity for the practice were allowed to study it at the academy.

When the wizard finished, Nick sagged forward and nearly took me down with him. Harvey side-stepped us to avoid getting crushed but didn't offer any help as I awkwardly lowered Nick to the ground. I looked up at the wizard, my eyes wide and alarmed. "Is that supposed to happen?"

The wizard shrugged. "He'll be fine." Without another word or further instruction, he sauntered off to join a cluster of agents at the other end of the parking lot.

"Harvey?"

"He'll be fine, Holly. I've seen this done dozens of times."

"Nick?" I shook his arm gently, then more frantically. His

expression was calm, no longer showing signs of fear or anxiety. He almost looked like he was merely sleeping. "Nick? Can you hear me?"

He stirred but his eyes remained closed. I looked to Harvey for some reassurance but he didn't say a word. He just continued to stare at Nick's motionless body. "Harvey, do something!"

Harvey heaved an impatient sigh. "He'll come around. Now, I have to go. He can't be here when he wakes up, so I suggest you use that necklace of yours and get him out of here."

One hand flew to the Larkspur. "You know about that?"

Harvey scoffed. "Of course we do, Holly. Honestly, sometimes I wonder what it is you think we do all day at the SPA." Harvey marched off to join the other agents without so much as a parting wave or smile.

Of course not.

I sighed and pulled the Larkspur from beneath my shirt. I'd never attempted to use it with another person and, despite Harvey's advice, I didn't feel confident that I could pull it off, especially after everything else that had transpired. I was wiped out and the last thing I needed was Nick coming to somewhere in the middle of nowhere without an explanation or a way home. So instead, I tucked the necklace back under my shirt and heaved Nick to his feet. He mumbled something under his breath but his eyes stayed shut. Considering our current surroundings, that was definitely for the best.

Just as I got him upright, a pair of headlights washed over us. I nearly cried with relief when Evangeline, Adam, and Lacey piled out of Evangeline's little sports car. Adam pounded the passenger seat as Lacey took her sweet time getting untangled. "Come on, princess. Hustle up!"

Lacey snarled at him but got out of the car and turned

back to fold down the seat so Adam could climb out of the back. Adam surged forward to get to me. He cupped my face and gave me a quick once-over before shifting his attention to Nick, who was still unconscious and propped up against my side. "What's up with Mr. Detective? One too many tequila shooters?"

"Tequila shooters?" Lacey scoffed. "He's obviously a bourbon man. Classy, sophisticated, older than his years. Stars, never mind. Look who I'm talking to. Those words probably don't even register with you, do they fluffy?"

Adam growled and Lacey gave him a triumphant smirk.

"What happened?" Evangeline asked, wisely ignoring the side show.

"He saw everything," I said weakly. "They had to wipe him."

They all gasped. "Wipe him?" Lacey asked, her tone suddenly hushed and hollow.

I nodded. "He hasn't woken up yet."

"Well let's get him back to the manor," Evangeline said, reaching to brace Nick's other side and take some of his weight from me. We all worked to get him into the backseat. "You getting in?" Evangeline asked me once he was situated.

I turned to look over my shoulder. I wanted to go back inside and see what was going on but I hated the idea of abandoning Nick after everything he'd been through.

Lacey placed her hand on my arm. "I'll get home. You take my seat. Make the fleabag babysit."

"Are you sure? Maybe I should go see if they need any help inside."

Lacey followed my glance and then shook her head. "Holly, you know they don't want you in there. They'll just tell you to leave and get out of their way. Whatever your deal was with Harvey, you've held up your end. It's time to let it go now."

I nodded as her words sank in. How could someone so shallow also be so pragmatic at times? "You're right. Thanks, Lacey." I tore my gaze away from the abandoned store front and glanced up into Lacey's shimmering eyes. "I hope there aren't any hard feelings. I know you were trying to help and I kinda made things worse for a minute there."

Lacey shrugged. "I'm looking at another few centuries on this earth, Holly. I prefer not to hold onto grudges for too long." She paused and looked over the top of the car to where Adam was standing. "I make an exception for him."

I laughed, thankful for the small bit of normalcy. "I've noticed."

She returned her gaze to me and smiled softly. "I'm grateful for your help, Holly. There's no telling what kind of damage Greyson and his followers would have done if you hadn't stepped in and stopped them. They weren't just bad for the vampire community, but for supernaturals in general. There was a time when I wouldn't have cared about anyone outside the vampire community, but now ..." She looked over at Adam and Evangeline and then back to me. "Now I have friends from all kinds of communities. Supernatural and not," she said, adding a meaningful glance at Nick.

Tears pricked at my eyes and I fought off the urge to pull her into a tight embrace. She might have finally admitted to being my friend, but if I tried to hug her she'd likely still try to claw my eyes out.

She returned my smile and then tossed her long blonde hair over her shoulders. "Come on, let's get back home. I'm right behind you. Posy will know what to do with him."

I gave her a grateful smile and slithered into the backseat to sit beside Nick. Adam locked the passenger seat in place and then got in after Lacey took off, using her super speed to nearly hover off the ground as she flew back in the direction of the manor.

CHAPTER 24

*H*alfway home, Nick began to stir. "Holly?" he mumbled, reaching for me.

"Nick! Oh, thank the stars! Can you hear me?"

His eyes fluttered slightly and then opened slowly. "Holly," he whispered, his lips curving into a smile. "You're here."

"Of course I am." I smoothed his unruly hair out of his eyes. "You had quite a fall."

At some point during the car ride, I'd decided that was the best cover for the situation.

"I did?" Nick asked as he tried to sit up.

I nodded. "Yeah. Are you dizzy or nauseated? Those were the signs we were supposed to look out for."

"We?" he repeated, looking around as if only just realizing his surroundings.

"Yeah, Evangeline and Adam are here too," I explained. Evangeline waved to him in the rear view mirror and Adam muttered a gruff *hey*. "What do you remember?"

He stared out the window for a long moment and then turned back to me. "Where are we?"

"On the way to the manor. Nick, please, try to remember," I urged, stopping short of shaking his arm. I knew it wouldn't be good if Nick suddenly recalled what we'd really been doing, but I could still hear the echoes of his pleas before the wiping and there was a part of me that wished he could be an exception to the SPA rules. That he could know the truth.

"There were bright lights, men with flashlights running around shouting."

Adam shifted around in his seat, suddenly perked up. His eyes met mine, wide and panicked.

"Holly?" Nick said, turning toward me. "Were we raided by the FBI? That's what the jackets said, right? FBI?"

Relief flooded Adam's eyes but I felt a sting of disappointment. "Yeah. They got the bad guys though. Don't you worry."

"That's good," Nick said. He sank back against the seat and his head slid over to land on my shoulder. "That's really good."

He fell back asleep and we didn't wake him until we got to the manor. Adam helped me get him inside and we put him on the couch in the living room and covered him with a thick flannel blanket before we all went to the kitchen. Lacey was already there, drinking straight from the bottle of faux blood. "Is he all right?" she asked as we all walked in slack-faced and exhausted.

I nodded. "He's asleep. He's fuzzy on the details but thinks it was an FBI raid. So I guess we're safe."

Adam glanced at Lacey on his way to his snack cupboard. "So keep those fangs to yourself there, princess."

She glared at him and then took another swig.

I started making a cup of tea even though I doubted I'd get halfway through it before succumbing to exhaustion. It felt like I hadn't slept in days. "Thanks for your help tonight," I started. "All of you."

"Of course, Holly," Evangeline said from her place at the kitchen table. "Friends don't let friends take on ancient vampire houses all alone."

I laughed. "Thank the stars for that."

Posy shimmered into sight through the kitchen door. "What's all the excitement about? And *who* is that on the couch out there?"

"It's a long story, Posy," I said, my voice tired and deflated. Steam poured off the water in the kettle and I poured a generous amount into my waiting mug.

"You know Holly," Adam told her as he crossed the kitchen, his arms full of snack foods. "Storming the castle and taking on the bad guys all in a fell swoop."

Posy raised her thick eyebrows. "Do I want to know?"

"Probably not," I said.

"Well, I do have some good news for the hero of the day," Adam said. "My parents have decided to leave a bit early. After all the excitement tonight, a goodbye brunch with them tomorrow should be no problem. Right, gorgeous?"

My spirits lifted considerably at that bit of news. I knew that something would have to give eventually, but I was glad that it was going to be off my plate for now. Still, I groaned and sank into my seat at the end of the table at the thought of even one more excruciating meal with them. "Truthfully, I'd rather deal with power-hungry vamps."

A chorus of laughter echoed around the room and then we all took turns giving Posy the rundown of the crazy night.

∿

THE FOLLOWING MORNING, I woke up and found the two guys eating cereal in the kitchen. Adam must have been coming around on Nick. After all, he didn't share his food with just anyone. The two of them looked comically relieved when I walked in. Adam jumped up and hurried to the cupboard. "You want a bowl, gorgeous?"

"What happened to brunch with your parents?" I asked, taking a seat at the table.

Nick smiled at me. "Oh, you haven't managed to scare them off yet?"

I laughed. "Someone's feeling better. And no. We're going to brunch in a bit. I thought," I added, looking at Adam's near-overflowing bowl. Then again, he'd be hungry again in ten minutes regardless.

"I'm feeling much better," Nick replied. "Thanks for taking care of me last night. Adam told me I had a little—okay, a lot—too much to drink."

I flapped a hand. "Don't mention it. It happens to all of us from time to time."

He chuckled and then shoveled in another bite of cereal—something chocolatey and named after a vampire from the looks of it. The irony struck me and I smiled across the kitchen at Adam. He shook the box at me and grinned mischievously back.

"It's weird how I don't remember any of it," Nick continued, his tone still dazed sounding. "It's not like me to drink heavily. I haven't gotten drunk since college."

I smiled sweetly at him and patted the back of his hand. "Well you're not as young as you once were."

Nick nodded but a conflicted look crossed his face. "I just wish I could remember. You ever have that feeling like you're forgetting something important?"

I held my breath. I didn't know much about how memory spells worked. Obviously the SPA knew what they were doing—they were a staple spell for their agents—but what if Nick was somehow fighting the spell?

"What's the last thing you remember?" Adam ventured.

"It's the weirdest thing, but I remember Georgia Banks called me—"

"She did?" My heart rocketed into my throat.

Adam shot me a play-it-cool look and I forced myself to swallow. "What—uh—what did she have to say?"

Nick struggled. "I don't—I can't remember. But if anyone could drive me to drink, it'd be her. I wish I could remember what she wanted …"

He gave a frustrated grunt and went back to eating his cereal. Adam and I exchanged a dark look over his head. Had Georgia called Nick and told him about Raven? I'd lost track of her in the crowd. She knew Nick and I worked together. Had she called him to warn him that I was in trouble? My heart squeezed at the thought. I made a mental note to call her and thank her for intervening, even though she'd inadvertently put Nick in danger.

"Man," Nick exclaimed. "It's like it's right there under the surface…"

I brushed my hand over his arm. "It's okay, Nick. Just let it go. I'm just glad we found you—" I looked up at Adam, waiting for him to fill in the half of the story he'd fed Nick.

"Outside your office," he supplied.

Right. I laughed. "You might have sent some pretty colorful emails in that state of mind."

Nick smiled over at me. "How do you always know what's going on around this town, Holly? You must have some kind of magic radar."

Adam and I exchanged a wry glance.

Nick glanced between us, a puzzled look on his face. "What? Come on, guys. It was just a joke."

A nervous laugh slipped from my lips and I jumped up from the table. "Well duh. Obviously you're joking."

Adam carried the box of cereal to the table as I reached

into the cabinet for a bowl. "Holly certainly has a knack for spotting trouble. I wouldn't necessarily call it *magical* though," he added.

I elbowed him in the ribs and stole the box from his hand. "Be nice or I'll make you go to brunch by yourself, then turn you into a dog."

Adam almost spewed a mouthful of cereal.

Nick chuckled at my *joke* as he polished off the rest of his breakfast. When his bowl was empty, I took it from him and deposited it into the sink.

"Thanks for breakfast," Nick said. "I should probably get home to shower and change. Let you get to your brunch," he added, giving me a knowing smile.

Evangeline breezed into the kitchen. "Oh, Nick! You're awake! How are you?"

"I'm doing good. Thanks."

"Hey, Evie, you mind if I snag your keys so we can drop Nick back at home?" Adam asked.

She nodded. "Sure. Or, I can take him. I think your parents are—" She paused as the door flapped open and Mort and Bella waltzed into the kitchen. "Awake."

Bats! So close …

"Morning guys," Adam said to his parents.

Evangeline backed toward the door. "Come on, Nick. I'll drive you home."

"Okay. Thanks again, guys. See you later."

Adam and I waved at him as he followed Evangeline out of the kitchen.

"You guys ready for brunch?" Adam asked, regardless of the fact that he'd just got done eating a serving bowl full of cereal.

Mort pocketed his hands. "Actually, son, we arranged an earlier flight, so we're going to go ahead and take off early. A cab's already on the way."

I moved to the sink to wash up the dishes—and hide my dramatic eye roll. Of course they were leaving earlier. It was ironic how moments before, I'd been dreading brunch but now, since they were actively opting out of it, I was offended.

"When is the cab—"

A ringtone interrupted Adam's question. Mort fished into his back pocket and retrieved a phone. "The cab's here."

I blinked. Wow. That was fast. They must really be in a hurry to get as far away from me as possible, although to be honest, I was just as eager for them to be gone. A surge of guilt swept through me at the thought and was quickly followed by a swell of sadness. I'd wanted Adam's parents to like me and approve of our relationship but it seemed that, at least for the time being, a general acknowledgment was about all I could expect.

Adam sighed and I craned around to see the frustrated look on his face. "All right," he said. "I guess so much for brunch."

Bella patted him on the shoulder. "It was just bad timing, honey. You obviously have a lot going on here." She looked over at me and I nearly lost my grip on the soapy bowl in my hands. "We'll try again next year."

Was that code for: you'll have found someone more suitable by then? I frowned into the sink full of dishes.

"Come on, I'll walk you out," Adam said.

I rinsed my hands and dried them on a dishtowel as I followed behind. Mort and Bella had their luggage neatly arranged by the front door and when Adam offered to help carry it to the cab, his dad waved him off. "Holly it was lovely to meet you," Mort said, giving me a slight nod.

Bella nodded in agreement, although her stony expression didn't quite match up with the sentiment.

"You too," I said, forcing a smile. "I'm sorry I was so busy while you were here."

Mort reached for the luggage and Adam got the door. While Adam said goodbye to his parents, I retreated back to the kitchen and finished the dishes. Once they were done, I went back to the living room and joined Adam at the large picture window as he waved goodbye. I looped my arm around him and dropped my head against his chest. "Well I don't know about you, but I'll tell you—I'm already *really* looking forward to next Thanksgiving."

Adam chuckled and wrapped an arm around my waist. "You know, I was thinking that maybe next year we should spend the holidays somewhere warm. Like Fiji."

I glanced up at him. "You're a genius."

"Fiji it is." He said and then pressed a kiss to my forehead. The cab pulled away from the curb and turned around in the cul-de-sac, before speeding off down the street. We each heaved a deep sigh and then moved away from the window and collapsed onto the couch.

"See," I said, wiggling to get comfortable. "If this was Fiji we'd be in a hammock right now, sipping some delicious cocktails with little pink umbrellas and listening to the ocean."

Adam chuckled. "I think you'd get bored."

"Really?"

He smiled down at me and took my hand. "I'm pretty sure that if you go a few weeks without stumbling into a crime scene, getting threatened with the possibility of being arrested, or being attacked by some undead creature, you'd go crazy."

I elbowed him playfully in the ribs. "Or, you could look at it this way: I just saved the entire haven system, and the planet in general, from a bunch of day-walking vampires with nearly unlimited resources and no regard for human life."

Adam laughed. "I suppose that's one way of looking at it. I guess I just didn't realize I was dating Wonder Woman."

"You think I need a theme song?" I asked, craning up to look at him.

"We'll work on it." He dropped a kiss to my forehead. "We've got time."

CHAPTER 25

"*Y*ou're sure you don't want me to come with you?"

I smiled at Adam's question—one he'd asked in one variation or another half a dozen times over the weeks leading up to the hearing date. "I'm sure. I don't know how long I'll be gone and I don't want you to miss out on any business."

He nodded understandingly, but the look on his face was still solemn. "What did you tell Cassie?"

"That I needed to use some of my vacation time to go back home for a visit. She didn't ask a lot of questions."

He pocketed his hands and shifted his weight between his feet.

"What's going on in that pretty little head of yours?" I teased.

"Just antsy I guess."

I knelt on the floor and waved my hand in the direction of my tried-and-true suitcase. It slithered out from under the bed and with another flick of my wrist, it floated up and landed on the bed with a soft *plop*. The arrangements were all in place. I had a hotel room at a swanky hotel in the heart of the Seattle haven. It would be my first trip back in over a year and I was flooded with different emotions. If Adam thought he was antsy, he needed to take a tour through my crowded mind. Teddy's petition to the Haven Council had worked and, with any luck, I would be leaving the haven with my master potion license.

I smiled up at Adam as I unzipped the suitcase. "It'll all work out. At least that's what Teddy says. Evangeline says he's a real shark and has a near perfect record when it comes to cases before the Council. He doesn't see any reason they could block my request. After all, I wasn't the one who was convicted in that whole mess with Gabriel."

Adam nodded. "I'm sure he knows what he's talking about," he agreed. "He seems very competent."

I grinned at Adam's odd compliment. Teddy was about as polar opposite from Adam as I could imagine. During his brief visit to the manor, they'd struggled to find much to talk about besides the weather. Adam didn't have an appreciation of designer suits and expensive loafers and premium hair products, and Teddy didn't have the first clue as to the rules of a football game or why anyone would wear black leather.

"The only thing that matters is that I get my license and can start my business back up again. You wouldn't believe the amount of phone calls I've been getting lately! Everyone is panicking and asking for recommendations on where else to go. I can't wait to get back and make the rounds to let everyone know I'm back!"

Adam chuckled. "I'm happy for you, Holly."

"Thanks." I went to the dresser and started gathering stacks of clothing. Teddy hadn't been able to tell me exactly how long the proceedings would take so I was planning ahead with at least a week's worth of clothing. Worst case scenario, I could jet back to the manor the following weekend or maybe beg something off my friend Anastasia Winters. We'd already made plans to get lunch together once I was in the city.

I smiled to myself as I grabbed up different outfits. Amid the fear that things wouldn't go as buttercream-smooth as Teddy predicted was the tiny ball of hope that I was about to be handed back the keys to my freedom. My life.

"So I guess in addition to getting your license, you won't be banished anymore, huh?"

I straightened, a t-shirt dangling from my hands. "I hadn't really thought of that, but yeah. I guess you're right. The only reason Harvey forced me out of the Seattle haven in the first place was to keep me from getting tossed back in jail for running my underground potion business."

"It's cute how you use the term *underground* instead of illegal," Adam teased.

I laughed as I crossed back to the bed and tucked the t-shirt into my suitcase. "Hardy har."

Adam pocketed his hands. "So then what's the plan? You'll still come back here, won't you?"

I stopped packing and met his eyes. "Of course, Adam. Why would you even ask that?"

He shrugged and lowered onto the side of the bed. "Your dream has always been to have your own potion shop. That can't happen here in Beechwood Harbor."

"Well no, not in the traditional sense, I suppose." I pulled my hair back into a low ponytail and secured it with an elastic band. "But I can go back to how it was before Harvey showed up. Except without the constant paranoia of an SPA raid."

Adam chuckled. "I guess so. But Holly, are you sure that's gonna be enough for you?"

"What's this really about, Adam? I get this feeling that you're not asking me the *real* question here."

He reached for me and I rounded the bed to sit beside him. "I know the whole visit with my parents was more interrogation and interview than peaceful family reunion. And for that, I'm truly sorry. I guess that ever since they showed up, things between us have been a little weird and now you're leaving, and I guess I'm just a little concerned."

"Wait a second! The infamous lady killer Adam St. James is feeling insecure?" I teased gently.

Adam chuckled. "I suppose it was bound to happen eventually. You must be pretty damned special, Holly Boldt."

I squeezed his hand and told him truthfully, "I feel pretty special."

Adam cupped the side of my face and for a long moment, neither of us said a word. When he broke the silence, his voice was low and hoarse. "I love you, Holly. I don't want to lose you."

"I love you, too, Adam. You're not going to lose me. I'm coming right back as soon as the hearing is over. I promise. It's going to take a lot more than Mort and Bella to scare me off."

Adam shook his head in disbelief. "How did I get so lucky?"

I scoffed.

"No, I'm serious, Holly. After all my parents' bad behavior, most women would have run for the hills."

"Most *sane* women, you mean."

He laughed and dropped a kiss to my lips. Gentle and sweet. My lashes fluttered against my cheeks as I closed my eyes and let myself get lost in the moment. "I've never been happier to have nabbed a crazy one then."

"How romantic. You should put that on my Valentine's Day card."

Adam kissed me again, his smile pressed to mine. "I'll think about it."

"Good." We lingered there on the bed, side by side, and the longer we stared at each other, the more my heart twisted inside my chest. I was only going to be gone for a week. Two at the most. Why was I so torn up over the idea of leaving Adam? The answer echoed back almost immediately. I was afraid that as soon as I got back to the Seattle haven, I would be homesick all over again and want to stay.

It had taken months to adjust to life in Beechwood Harbor and while I'd become convinced it was my new home, and possibly what I'd been searching for since leaving California, there was a tiny piece of me that missed the glitter and rush of living in a big city. In Beechwood Harbor I would always be known as Holly the potions witch. But what if I wanted more than that? Adam was right. Having my own potions shop had always been the goal. And now ... I'd never been closer. It wouldn't be like before. I wouldn't be forced to work as an apprentice, barely authorized to chop basil or cattails. I could be a master potion maker with my own shop and custom blends that would be sought out all over the supernatural world.

In Beechwood Harbor, the largest reach I had would probably be less than three counties.

"Holly? You okay?" Adam asked, running his fingers along the side of my face. He circled my ear, tucking away a flyaway strand of hair that had escaped from my ponytail.

I snapped out of my reverie and nodded, then tried to summon a convincing smile. "Yeah. Uh, what time is it?" I asked, leaning past Adam to get a look at the clock on the opposite night stand. "I need to get to the haven portal in about an hour. Harvey was nice enough to get me a special pass to use it. He said it will be unlocked for me to use but he was very particular about the time for some reason."

"An hour, huh?" Adam stood from the bed and reached

for my hands. "Sounds like the perfect amount of time for a snack."

I laughed. "Tell me something, Adam. Is there ever *not* time for a snack?"

He didn't answer as he led me from the room and down the stairs and into the kitchen. As soon as the door flapped open, I could see that Evangeline, Lacey, and Posy had all gathered around the large table. A spread of my favorite treats—including a double-decker Lemon Cloud cake, complete with tiny, lemon-shaped sprinkles in the whipped cream—adorned the table.

I clapped a hand to my mouth for a moment. "What's all this?"

Adam grinned. "Just a little going away buffet. Nothing too crazy."

"You guys!" I gushed, nearly on the verge of tears. "It's just a week or two!"

Posy floated forward. "Yes, dear, but you're the heart of this place. We're all going to miss you, no matter how short of a time it ends up being."

I swallowed the lump of emotion in my throat. "Thank you, Posy."

Evangeline smiled. "You're going to kick butt, Holly. I can't wait until you're back in business so we can see what you come up with! I've already got all the girls at the salon ready for our second line of hair products."

"You got it!"

Lacey smiled at me. "I'm just here in case you get yourself thrown back in SPA jail and we never see you again."

Everyone laughed and I rushed forward and gave her a hug before she could object.

"All right, ladies. Enough of this sappy stuff. Let's get to business," Adam interjected. He slapped his hands together and rubbed them vigorously. "Let's eat!"

Once all of the food was gone and the goodbyes were said, I went upstairs to finish packing. Adam lugged my suitcase down the stairs while I rounded up Boots and enough cans of food to keep him happy during the trip.

Adam walked with me to the portal dragging my suitcase behind him and I was reminded of my last trip down the same streets. I'd been locked in magically enhanced handcuffs and I was the one being carted behind Harvey. I shuddered at the memory and the emotions it stirred.

"It's down here," I said, pointing to the house with the cellar doors. There were lights on in the front room of the house and for a moment I wondered who lived there. Harvey had never mentioned them by name. Beechwood Harbor was small enough that I would probably recognize them, but then again, they had a portal to the haven right under their house; they probably didn't deal with the locals much. They were probably content to be the mysterious guardians of the portal.

"It's strange, but I can't remember ever seeing this house before," Adam commented as we neared it.

"The portal is on the right."

We approached the portal and Adam set my suitcase down in the frost-covered grass. He gathered me against him and gave me a lingering kiss. "Stay outta trouble," he said when we parted.

I grinned. "Planning on it."

I reached for the handle of the cellar door and pulled it open. As before, the faint purple glow shone from the opening and a shiver of excitement snaked down my spine. "This is it."

"Here," Adam said as he bent and picked up my suitcase.

I scooped Boots into my arms and the tabby stared, mesmerized, into the purple beyond. "You ready, Bootsie? For our next grand adventure?"

He looked up at me and blinked once. I took it as a yes.

"Hey, Holly."

I turned back. "Huh?"

Adam flashed a goofy grin. "I hope you don't run into any vampires."

"You and me both!" I replied with a laugh.

"Good luck, gorgeous," he whispered, touching my face.

I nodded and then took a deep breath and one big step.

AUTHOR'S NOTE: Thank you so much for reading Witch Slapped. I have to say, this was one of my favorites to write! I hope you enjoyed it just as much. Holly's tale continues in the next book, Witch Way Home.

If you'd like to get exclusive short stories, bonus content, and the first look at all upcoming projects, be sure to join my reader's list. You can go to www.DanielleGarrettBooks.com/newsletter and sign up today and receive the prequel novella A Witch of a Day completely free.

I hope to see you in the harbor again, really soon!

Until then,

Danielle Garrett

ACKNOWLEDGMENTS

First of all, I would like to thank my parents, who fed my love of reading from an early age. My sister, for supporting my desire to tell stories since I started "over complicating" our Barbie doll's lives.

For my handsome husband, you know how much I love you. I appreciate your daily support (and for listening to all of my writerly rants and keeping my caffeinated at all times).

Thank you to Theresa, my fabulous editor for all of your tips and kind words. And Keri, for the killer covers.

Writing can be a solitary passion, but with all of you beside me, it's never lonely.

Thank you.

ABOUT DANIELLE GARRETT

From a young age, Danielle Garrett was obsessed with fantastic places and the stories set within them. As a lifelong bookworm, she's gone on hundreds of adventures through the eyes of wizards, princesses, elves, and some rather wonderful everyday people as well.

Danielle now lives in Oregon and while she travels as often as possible, she wouldn't want to call anywhere else home. She shares her life with her husband and their house full of animals, and when not writing, spends her time being a house servant for three extremely spoiled cats and one outnumbered puppy.

For more about Danielle and her work, please visit her at:
www.daniellegarrettbooks.com
www.facebook.com/daniellegarrettbooks

CPSIA information can be obtained
at www.ICGtesting.com
Printed in the USA
LVOW12s1315181217
560164LV00005B/456/P